MW00947673

This Much Is True

Adriana Locke

This Much Is True
Copyright © 2023 Adriana Locke
All rights reserved

No part of this publication may be reproduced, distributed, or transmitted in any form or by any means, including photocopying, recording, or other electronic or mechanical methods, without the prior written consent of the publisher, except in the case of brief quotations embodied in critical reviews and certain other noncommercial uses permitted by copyright law.

Cover Design: Kari March, www.karimarch.com

Photographer: Wander Aguiar, Wander Aguiar Photography LLC

Editor: Marion Archer, Marion Making Manuscripts

Editor: Jenny Simms, Editing 4 Indies

Proofreader: Michele Ficht

Books by Adriana Locke

My Amazon Store

Brewer Family Series
The Proposal | The Arrangement

Carmichael Family Series
Flirt | Fling | Fluke | Flaunt | Flame

Landry Family Series
Sway | Swing | Switch | Swear | Swink | Sweet

Landry Family Security Series
Pulse

Gibson Boys Series
Crank | Craft | Cross | Crave | Crazy

The Mason Family Series
Restraint | The Relationship Pact | Reputation | Reckless | Relentless | Resolution

The Marshall Family Series
More Than I Could | This Much Is True

The Exception Series
The Exception | The Perception

For a complete reading order and more information, visit www.adrianalocke.com.

Synopsis

When celebrity Laina Kelley bolted from her small hometown church on her wedding day, she ran to the first place that came to mind—to the home of the local farrier, a gorgeous playboy who just so happens to be her first love ... and biggest frenemy.

USA Today bestselling author Adriana Locke delivers a new "sweet and spicy!" standalone romance about a runaway bride who finds herself in the horse barn, and arms, of her deliciously handsome frenemy —who just so happens to be her first love.

This isn't your average romance. It begins with me in a wedding dress, just not at an altar ...

I never expected to be a runaway bride. I also never thought I'd end up on my ex's doorstep to flee from my wedding. However, I'm here, and it's easy to find the key in an old boot by the door and let myself in. It's not breaking and entering if I have a key, right?

It's safe to say that Luke Marshall didn't expect to find me on his couch in my wedding dress. He has no choice but to listen to my panic-induced plea for refuge. It's only a matter of time before the tabloids get wind of my disappearing act, and then? My life as I know it is over.

Luke takes pity on me and says I can stay... on one condition.

I can't sing for my supper. I have to earn it. *In the barn.* I'll be up to my elbows in horse manure. And because there's only one bed, I get the couch.

This works ... in theory. But when sparks start flying, I'm offered a permanent place to stay—in his arms forever. I'll have to decide between my life as a pop star and a second chance with my first love.

Chapter One

L aina

"What do you mean you're on the run?"

Stephanie's question is valid, as is her curious but mostly nonchalant way of asking it. After all, it's me we're talking about. But she should've been more prepared.

"Do I really need to break it down for you—*darn it!*" I pry my heel out of a slit in the asphalt. "Besides, when your best friend calls and says she's on the run and needs your help, the only question you should ask is *whose car are we taking?*"

"You're *so* funny."

I glance to my right, then to my left. A trail of sweat trickles between my shoulder blades. Aside from two men in fitted suits and sunglasses from the security team, I'm in the clear.

"There's nothing funny about this," I say, darting across the parking lot as gracefully as possible despite the layers of tulle.

"The last time I saw you—which was approximately fifteen minutes ago, give or take—you were in your wedding dress, looking

1

stunning, I might add, waiting for your father to show up to walk you down the aisle."

Fifteen minutes? Man, I work quick.

The crowd roars from the other side of the safety barrier Landry Security erected three days ago to keep fans and paparazzi—mostly paparazzi—away from the church. Brickfield has been teeming all week with spectators eager to see what the media has deemed the wedding of the century. Former classmates were interviewed. My kindergarten teacher was on the front page of *Exposé* magazine this week. Alleged encounters with the "men in my life" since I became famous have been dissected and analyzed to death. If only half of what was printed were real, my life would be far more entertaining.

I would've felt bad for Sheriff Jones in his plight to organize a response to this level of anarchy in a town of five thousand people if he hadn't used my wedding as the launch of his re-election campaign.

"What's going on, Laina? Are you joking around, or is something really the matter?"

"Considering I'm currently hiding between two sheds and hoping no one is flying drones overhead, I'd say something is the matter."

"Why are you between two sheds?"

I spit a piece of my veil out of my face. "I can't marry him, Steph."

My best friend goes silent. I imagine her face—mouth agape, brows arched higher than the lamination treatment should allow, and a wrinkled forehead defying her Botox. She wore the same expression when I told her I was marrying Hollywood heartthrob Tom Waverly a year ago—complete and utter shock.

"I should've listened to you," I say, taking a steadying breath. "I never should've accepted his proposal at all, let alone plan a wedding and invite one hundred fifty people to the church and another two hundred to a reception that cost more than ..." Dread rolls through the pit of my stomach. "Let's not even go there."

"Okay." Her voice is cool and tempered. "What do you need?"

"Ironically enough, I need you to ask whose car we're taking because the answer is *I don't know*. I didn't think this through. I excused myself from the room, shut the door, and left."

"We're throwing a plot twist at the last second, but that's okay. I think quick on my feet, so don't panic."

"Strangely, I'm not. I don't know whether that's because I'm blocking out the ramifications of this wholly impulsive decision or if this is my gut's way of thanking me for following it." I peer around the side of one of the sheds, nearly getting busted by the best man. "I'll take it either way."

"We're going with the latter. Now, where are you, exactly?"

"Behind the church. There are two sheds with a hedgerow behind them. I'm between the buildings."

The crowd roars once again. But instead of the ordinary screams and whistles, they begin to sing the chorus of the most popular song on country radio.

"Guess Sam's here," I say, sighing.

"Don't worry about who is here. Let's worry about getting you out of here."

"Therein lies my problem." I nibble the lip stain that took me six months to pick out. "People are everywhere. I can't just walk out the gate and onto the street. I get recognized in a wig, hat, and sunglasses, let alone a freaking wedding dress."

My heart pounds as the weight of my actions sinks in.

Tom will be humiliated. The biggest movie star in the world will be left standing at the altar by the pop star the world is quick to label *frivolous*. My parents' fury will be immeasurable. *How dare I be so careless with my image when so much of their success is riding on it?* My PR team will be inundated with calls and emails. My assistant *must* stay out of sight until this cools down, and my fans will jump to conclusions and assume the worst about me. *About Tom.* Critics will claim this was a publicity stunt when it's nothing more than a woman trying to salvage her future amid a few bad choices.

"Maybe I should just go through with it," I say, a chill prickling my skin. "The ramifications of this—"

3

"It's ten years from now, and you're on a beach."

"Can we talk about vacations later?"

"And you look to your left, and there's Tom," she says. "How do you feel?"

Sick.

Uneasiness stirs in my stomach. Instead of imagining Tom gazing adoringly back at me, I instantly notice the angry lines around his eyes. His voice sweeps through my head.

"There are calories in those drinks, you know."

"We're going to have to talk about you easing up on the music thing when I start filming my next project in the winter."

"Can't you choose more conservative costumes? You're a grown woman, for fuck's sake. I don't want my wife out there looking like a whore."

I grapple with how to phrase that, but Stephanie saves me the trouble.

"Now imagine that you look to the left, and he's gone," she says. "How do you feel now?"

Peaceful.

Relief eases the tension in my shoulders and quells the knot in my stomach. I don't try to answer her this time; it's unnecessary.

"The ramifications of going back in that church and marrying Tom are far worse than the inconvenience it will cause everyone else if you don't," she says. "I'll support you either way. But your father was just in here looking for you, and while I can stall him for a little bit, you need to decide."

A shiver runs the length of my spine. A flush stings my cheeks. My heart somehow lodges in my throat, and each beat reminds me of the seconds ticking by.

I can't do it. I can't return to that church and walk out as Mrs. Tom Waverly. The thought makes me want to hurl.

"The media will have a heyday with this," I say, my back pressed against the shed. "I can see the headlines already."

4

"Ignore all of that. You're going to wake up married or not. What's it going to be?"

My breath quickens. "I'm not."

"You're sure."

"Yes."

A door closes in the background. "Okay, this is the plan."

A smile tugs at my lips.

"I could borrow a car and pick you up, but someone has to be here to head off your parents and Tom until you've made your exit," she says. "The security team is our best bet, I think. They're under an NDA, and you hired them, right? Not Tom?"

"Yeah, I did."

"Okay. Let me find one of them and get them to pick you up. You stay put. I'm going to bide you some time with your father. Who should I contact on your team?"

"My agent. Anjelica Grace at Mason Music," I say. "Tell her I'll call her as soon as I can."

"I'm on it. Do you need me to do anything else?"

I take a long breath. "Don't be the one to tell Tom. Let someone else do it."

"Got it. Now, hold tight. I'll have a car there as fast as I can."

"I love you, Steph."

"Love you more."

"Oh! And my engagement ring is in your purse."

"Got it."

The call ends. I drop my arm to the side and avoid looking at the phone screen. People are probably already sending texts and looking for me. I can't deal with it. Not yet.

I'm really doing this. I'm really running away from my wedding.

My head begins to spin with all the immediate decisions I must make. I have to get my things from the hotel before it's taken over by the wedding party again. *Can anyone track my phone? How will I get out of here without alerting the media and bystanders?*

Is that even possible?

Before I can go too far down the rabbit hole, a black SUV rolls up perilously close to the shed. The windows are jet black, making it impossible to see inside. Nerves ripple low in my stomach as a man in one of those tailored suits slips alongside the vehicle.

He takes his glasses off so I can see his gray eyes. *Troy Castelli. Thank God.*

"Ms. Kelley, I heard you'd like a ride."

A chuckle escapes me. "I can't believe I'm doing this, Troy."

"I'm happy to take you wherever you want."

"I just want to get out of here without my picture being splashed on social media. Can you pull that off?"

He opens the back door. "Absolutely." He turns to offer me a hand and then sees, for what seems like the first time, the tulle that must also go in the SUV. "How do we get all of ... *that* in there?"

"It's tulle." I bunch as much of the fabric in the front as I can. "I hate it."

"Then why did you choose it?"

The question makes me pause. *Why did I choose tulle over lace? Surf-n-turf over chicken strips and sliders for the reception? The diet drink over the full sugar soda at the rehearsal dinner?*

"Troy, it seems I'm a bit of a pushover."

"No offense, ma'am, but a lot of people inside the church would probably disagree with you."

I grin, standing a little taller. "You're right. Now shove this godforsaken dress in the car, and let's get out of here."

With a little work and a lot of pushing white fabric into every vacant space in the back of the SUV, we make it work. Troy is in the driver's seat in the blink of an eye.

"We'll go out the back service entrance," he says, holding my gaze in the rearview mirror. "You can breathe, Ms. Kelley. It's going to be all right."

I exhale, the sound taking up all the room the tulle isn't. *I hope you're right.*

My heart pounds as we roll to the back of the church. Troy makes a hand signal to a police officer at the makeshift gate, and it's immediately moved.

The crowd has nearly tripled since I arrived two hours ago. The streets have been closed, and people have filled the block surrounding Mt. Calvary Church. Lawns of the nearby houses are littered with bodies. Television crews are set up on sidewalks with vans and microphones.

It's a mess.

And about to get messier.

I glance at the clock on the dash. The ceremony is set to start in two minutes. I squeeze my eyes closed and try to ignore the fire blazing in my stomach.

"Ms. Kelly?"

I open my eyes. "Yes?"

"Where are we headed?"

Oh. Right.

Good freaking question.

Adrenaline flows through my veins, and my palms start to sweat. *Where* are *we headed?*

The hotel is out. The bridal party will inevitably return to their rooms to gather their things. Not to mention, there's no way I could get into the hotel discreetly and make it to my room. My parents' house is a definite no. I'd be emotionally *and* physically burned at the stake. I could ask Troy to drive me to the airport, but that's an hour and a half away, *and* no reservations have been made. My passport is at the hotel. *And what do I do with all this damn tulle?*

Breathe, Laina.

There must be somewhere I can go.

I sort through every person I still know in Brickfield—which isn't many. I've lost contact with nearly all my old friends since I left six years ago. I can't trust anyone to hide me until I figure this disaster out, anyway. I can't even get a room in Peachwood Falls because someone would wind up seeing me, and I'd get trapped with no way out.

"How about ..." Before I can ask him to find a back road to kill some time while I think, the answer pops in my head.

It is safe. *Probably.*

I may not exactly be welcome, but I won't be forced to leave. *I don't think.*

There will definitely be nothing to eat, the bedding will need to be washed, but I'll be able to let myself inside.

My lips curl slowly into a smile. And, for the first time today, I don't feel like the sun is setting on my soul.

"See that sign for Peachwood Falls?" I ask. "Head there."

Chapter Two

Laina

The asphalt, busted with potholes but asphalt all the same, turns into gravel. Troy slows the SUV as its tires crunch across the rocks.

The field on the right side of the road has a path leading to a smaller field in the rear. It's on top of a hill, surrounded by trees, and was too much of a pain in the ass to farm, according to the old farmer who used to tend to the land. My friends and I spent many weekend nights back there listening to music, building bonfires that almost got away from us, and drinking cheap wine and even cheaper beer like the adults we weren't.

If only we knew how overrated adulthood really was ...

On the left is a cornfield. A small brown home is tucked off the road. The family who lived there were so sweet. The father worked for the Department of Natural Resources and adopted a fawn that was left behind when its mother was shot during hunting season. The little thing would eat an apple out of your hand.

I wonder what happened to it.

"Just down this hill and around the curve," I say, shivering. *Why is it so chilly in here?* "The driveway is hard to see but on the right."

Troy nods. "Should I wait with you outside the house, or would you rather I wait down by the road?"

"With all due respect, I would rather you return to the church."

A frown darkens his face. "I'm sure you understand I can't do that, ma'am."

I hold his gaze in the rearview mirror, anger from being told what I can and can't do in my own damn life boiling inside me. But that's not Troy's fault. He's doing what he's paid to do.

And he's being paid by *me*.

"Look, I appreciate your concern and understand the challenge of returning without me," I say. "But I need a minute to myself, and *I really* need no one to know where I am for a while."

He watches me warily.

"Trust me. I don't want to get whacked by a crazed stalker more than you don't want me to be, okay?"

"I will have to tell my boss, Ms. Kelley."

Great.

My response is delayed as the SUV slows at the end of a small bridge crossing a creek. The driveway is next to a mailbox that's seen better days. We slip between the mailbox and guardrail and follow the bend around a hedge of trees.

And there it is.

My heart hammers against my rib cage as the yellow house with brown trim comes into view, its attached garage and large barn behind it. The lake below reflects the clear blue sky, and if I weren't running on adrenaline and eagerness to extract myself from this situation, I would appreciate the beauty and stillness of the moment.

The vehicle pulls to the top of the driveway and stops.

I stare at the door, wondering if he's home. *What will he say? What will he do?* Despite the chance that Luke Marshall won't be pleased to see me, my anxiety is the lowest it's been all day.

My shoulders slump against the seat.

"This is it?" Troy's sunglasses are gone, and he's surveying the landscape for threats. "Want me to walk the perimeter or, better yet, clear the inside?"

I sit up. "Promise me you won't tell Tom or my parents," I say, holding on to the back of the seat. "If you have to tell Ford Landry, then fine. But let him know that if he shares my location with anyone ... I'll fire you all."

His eyes blaze with frustration, but he heeds my request.

"Yes, Ms. Kelley."

I open the door handle, but nothing happens. Troy triggers the unlock feature and hops out of the driver's seat. When he's around to my side of the SUV, I'm gathering the tulle.

"I can stay out of sight," he says, clearly struggling with leaving me on a random doorstep. "I assure you that you won't know I'm here."

My bare feet hit the sharp rocks on the ground, and I wince. "Nope. I got this."

"I'll wait until you're inside."

"Nope." I square my shoulders to his. "*I got this.*"

He hesitates. "Call me if you need me. Do you have my number?"

"Yes. And, Troy? Thank you."

He mumbles something I can't hear, closes my door, and then goes to the other side. I quickly crack it open, turn my phone off, toss it onto the floorboard, and close the door again. My management's insistence that I memorize my most important phone numbers is finally coming in handy.

As he drives off, rounding the turn and effectively going out of sight, I blow out the deepest, heaviest breath of my life.

I face the house that holds so many memories. The walkout basement that Luke and I used when we didn't want his grandfather, Poppy Marshall, to know we were there. The birdbath next to the house has a permanent crack down the side because Luke hit it with his truck one winter while sliding on the ice. I glance at the front porch. And the old pair of boots behind the porch swing—the one with the house key.

"Ouch," I hiss, stepping lightly on the gravel toward the stairs.

My mind drifts away, carrying me back to the situation at the church. How is Stephanie handling the drama? I envision the statement Tom is composing for the press. *He's undoubtedly feeding me to the wolves.* It takes little imagination to picture my parents' displeasure. *Did they outright take Tom's side, or do they wonder, if even for a moment, what my side of the story might be?*

Tears flood my eyes, fogging my sight.

If I had stayed, I'd be a married woman right now.

My hands shake as if I've just avoided being mugged.

The thought of cutting it so close—almost being Mrs. Tom Waverly—makes me nauseous. Even though I'll undoubtedly be on the receiving end of nasty vitriol in the coming days, it's a small price to pay for avoiding a marriage that would've ended in divorce. Tom may not understand it, but I did us both a favor.

I grab the rail and pull the tulle behind me up the stairs. Poppy's standing ashtray from decades ago is still next to the swing. The sight of it surrounded by the ridiculous white fabric makes me grin.

I press the doorbell and wait. There's no movement inside the house. I press it again.

My heart pounds as I dip my hand into the right boot.

"So predictable, Luke," I say, pulling out the spare key. I stick it in the lock, and the door swings open as if waiting for me. The thought makes me smile.

The hardwood is warm on my bare feet. An earthiness unique to this place—mud mixed with tobacco and kissed by the sun—greets me like an old friend. I shut the door behind me and venture into Luke's house.

A bigger television hangs on the wall. The refrigerator has been replaced. A few more pictures have been added to the collection of family photos on the unused dining room table. Not much has changed in the six years since I was here. Yet ...

Every move I make is like a pin dropping to the floor. It's as if the house is holding its breath like me. Somehow, it feels like I just came in after a shift at The Scoop to do homework with Luke.

My dress swishes against the floor as I cross the kitchen to inspect the photographs.

So many framed memories have been here for years—pictures of Poppy and Luke's grandma and Luke's parents. There are photos of Luke and his siblings. My favorite one is in the center of the table, and I pick it up.

Luke gives the camera the cheesiest grin. To his right are his oldest brothers, Chase and Mallet. On his left is his little sister, Kate. Crouched in front of them, as if he might attack the person taking the shot, is their brother Gavin. *God, I love these people.*

It's hard to breathe as I gaze at the faces I haven't seen in a long time—faces of some of the best, most hardworking, salt-of-the-earth people I've ever met. They loved me like their own. I loved them right back. Until everything fell apart ...

I wipe away the tears rolling down my cheeks and set the picture back in its place.

"I shouldn't be here," I whisper, looking around the house. "What am I doing?"

Panic surges, using the crack in my willpower to make itself known. My stomach clenches like I might puke. Fight-or-flight instincts kick in. My brain screams at my legs to move, to walk—to leave before I make a mess of things, but my heart whispers *no*.

There's nowhere else to go, anyway.

I'm royally screwed.

I sit on the brown plaid couch. The springs bite through all the fabric attached to my butt and bite into my bones. At least I can feel it. At least I'm not *that* numb.

Gravel popping under the weight of a vehicle rings through the silence. I bolt upright, unsure whether to run out the back door or sit still and take whatever comes my way. For the briefest of seconds, I regret asking Troy to leave.

A door shuts. Boots climb the stairs. The handle turns, the hinges creaking.

I grab the edge of the couch, holding my breath and waiting for my eyes to meet Luke Marshall's.

When he enters, his head is down. He shuts the door with his foot. With his phone in his hand, he lifts his face and stops mid-step.

The phone clatters to the floor.

I gasp as our gazes collide, and the world outside this room ceases to exist. The collision takes my breath as heat sizzles through my body, snaking down my spine in a slow, torturous curl.

I struggle to catch my breath amid the butterflies sweeping through my stomach.

Oh, my ...

Luke Marshall is all grown up.

Age has done fine things to this man, filling him out in all the right places—broad shoulders and a barrel chest. A belt shows off his trim waist. Angled jaw. *Long lashes.* He wears a day's scruff that makes me shiver.

No amount of social media stalking could've prepared me for this moment.

He tilts his head in surprise, then in confusion.

A sardonic smile parts his kissable lips. "What in the hell are you doing here?"

Chapter Three

Laina

His voice—playful and rich with a hint of mischief—
sweeps across the room. It's as if a fuse is extinguished, and my world
has stopped careening toward the edge of a cliff. I breathe freely for
the first time in days.

"Hey, Luke," I say.

He scratches the top of his head, then runs his palm down the
side of his cheek. His mouth opens, and he takes a breath like he's
going to speak. Instead, he chuckles.

Relief rolls off me in waves.

"Aren't you supposed to be getting married today?" he asks, a
teasing quirk at the corner of his mouth.

"I'm not sure what would give you that impression."

He lifts a brow, keeping an eye on me while he picks his phone
off the floor. "I don't know. Could be the wedding dress. Might be
your pictures and the word *wedding* splashed all over the news. Then
again, it could be all the assholes in fancy suits sitting around The
Wet Whistle talking about the economy and not even having the

courtesy to laugh at Tucker's jokes." He tosses the phone on the table beneath the television. "You choose."

"I'll go with the assholes in fancy suits. But *I* didn't invite them. They are here by invitation from the groom."

"Speaking of the groom, why aren't you with him again?"

My insides still as we watch each other.

Once upon a time, I could peer into those beautiful green eyes and know exactly what he was thinking. And I wouldn't dare look at him if I didn't want him to read me like a book. But his gaze now holds stories we don't share, experiences I don't understand, and wounds I didn't heal. The difference cuts me to the quick.

Just as my heart races, he flashes me his crooked smile.

I sigh, fighting a smile of my own. "I kind of left him at the altar."

"Ballsy way to start a marriage."

"Yeah, it would be if we were starting one."

He leans against the wall, and a faint smirk kisses his lips. "I have so many questions."

"I bet you do."

He holds my gaze for a moment and then stands tall. "Let's start with the most important one."

I brace myself, expecting him to ask why I left my wedding.

"Is anyone coming here looking for you?" he asks.

What? "Why? Did you see someone?"

A sweaty palm falls to my chest in a futile attempt at discouraging a swell of panic from rising. In my failure to plan this adventure, it never occurred to me that I might be dragging Luke into an uncomfortable position. After all, he didn't ask for this.

"I'm sorry," I say, getting to my feet. "I shouldn't have come here. I didn't think—"

"Sit down, Pumpkin." His eyes twinkle. "You talk too much when you're nervous."

My chest burns, lingering on my nickname from when we were younger. I sit as requested and struggle to catch my breath.

"I don't want to bring you into this," I say.

"Looks like it's a little too late for that." He smirks. "You're safe here. You know that."

Every muscle relaxes, and I sink into the most uncomfortable couch in the universe. But it doesn't matter how many springs poke my butt. It doesn't matter if Luke can protect me—or if he should. The only thing that matters is that he would try. Even after all these years, he would still offer me refuge. I can count on him.

I grin. *Just like I knew I could.*

"Seriously, though," he says, lifting a brow. "I imagine there's a pissed-off movie star with a security team straight out of a combat zone searching Peachwood County for a runaway bride right about now. It's not that I couldn't take them. I'm just wondering if I need to call for reinforcements."

I laugh. "If by reinforcements you mean Gavin, you might be better off on your own. I remember when Gavin played dead in the mud pits instead of helping you talk to the police about why we were out there past dark."

Luke laughs, too, and disappears around the corner. "I haven't thought about that in a long time."

"I can't think of Gavin and not think about it."

"Serves him right to have that as his legacy. Little shit." Ice clinks against a glass. "Back to the topic at hand. Does anyone know you're here?" He pokes his head around the corner. "Why *are* you here, anyway?"

My throat goes dry, and I'm suddenly aware of every rise and fall of my chest. He watches me for the longest time, giving me a chance to answer. Finally, a shadow falls across his face, and he disappears again.

"Let's back up," he says, rounding the corner with two glasses of tea. "How the hell did you get in my house to start with?"

"Key in the boot."

"How'd you know about that?"

I take the glass from him. "I'm the one who put the key in the boot the first time. I created that hiding spot. I just took a chance that you are a creature of habit and struck gold."

"Damn. I probably oughta move that, huh?"

"Might not be a bad idea." *Especially if some of his other exes turn up out of the blue.* Can't say I love that idea. Strangely.

He sits on the chair across the coffee table and takes a drink. I wonder what he's thinking with that glimmer in his eye, but I don't ask. I'm not exactly in the driver's seat.

The sun streams in the windows, filling the living room with a bright warmth that seeps into every corner. This house has always had a tranquility about it. Before Poppy passed away and we'd come here so Luke could help his grandfather in the barn, it was always so peaceful. No matter the stress at home, or drama at school, or worries about whatever deal my father was trying to make on my behalf, it all melted away in this house.

"Okay, so let me get this straight," Luke says. "You're not getting married and fled the scene. Then you showed up here, performed a felony to get into my house, and now ... what?"

I smile sheepishly. "I kind of ... *don't* have a plan."

"So you just tied me up in one of your shenanigans that will be one of the year's biggest scandals. Awesome."

"Oh, don't act like you don't love a good shenanigan."

"Not the point," he says, grinning. "I also love a good tie-up, but that's not the point either."

My stomach muscles contract at the heat in his gaze. "I didn't know where else to go."

"Hey, it's not bad for my ego that I was the only person you could think of when you were running from Tom fucking Waverly."

I smirk. "I said I couldn't think of anywhere else to go. Not *who else.*"

"*Okay.*" He rolls his eyes. "How many houses do you own again?"

"How did you say it? *Not the point.*"

We exchange a small smile that fills me with big emotions— namely, comfort.

Luke and I could've been a perfect match in another time and place.

I've replayed the day we broke up more times than I've replayed any other event of my life. That moment impacted me more than any charity work, music award, or concert I've ever performed. A sunny afternoon, Luke in black-and-yellow flannel, standing in his parents' driveway. Luke didn't ask me to stay with him, and I didn't ask him to go. It's haunted me ever since. But after each review, I'm left with the same conclusion: it ended the only way it could've.

I rest my glass on my dress as a lump rises in my throat. "I can't go to any of my homes. Tom's team is crafting his image-saving statement as we speak, and it will not do me any favors. The paparazzi will case my houses and the airport. They'll even dispatch reporters to places they *think* I might go."

"Where are you going to go?"

I gulp. "I don't know. Maybe I could stay here?"

The words fly out of my mouth before I can stop them. *Before I can think them through.* My brain forms sentences and tells my lips to say them, to backtrack my word vomit and save face. But my heart, *my stupid, stupid heart*, blockades the effort.

My chest burns with anticipation as I watch Luke take a piece of gum from his pocket, put it into his mouth, and chew deliberately. His gaze holds mine with suspicion, fire, and something else I can't quite name. The mixture feeds the pang in my chest.

"I think you staying here would be the worst idea you've ever had," he says after a long pause. "And you've had some epically shitty ones."

"Now you're just being a dick."

"Want me to rattle off a few? Fine," he says before I can answer. "You bought a car from a man known as Lemonade Larry because all he sold was lemons."

"Okay, but you tried to drag race a cop. That's even dumber."

"You tried to polar plunge in Peachwood Creek in a bikini and ended up falling on the ice and giving yourself a concussion."

"Fine, but you ran butt naked through the middle of town to celebrate the football team going to the state finals and got blackmailed by a stranger who may or may not have had pictures of you performing the Electric Slide on Main Street in nothing but a jock strap."

He narrows his eyes. "There was alcohol involved."

I narrow mine right back. "Like that's an excuse."

Slowly, our lips curve into a smile, and before we know it, we're laughing.

"Can I stay?" I ask.

"No. You'll cramp my style."

"You don't *have* a style."

He takes out another piece of gum and pops it into his mouth.

"I'll pay rent," I say as sweetly as possible.

"*Rent?* How long are you talking about? I have a life, you know."

"I told you—I didn't plan this out."

"Clearly." He gets to his feet and moves to the kitchen doorway. "I can't take you seriously in that thing."

"In what thing?"

His eyes scan the length of me. "It's so ... fluffy."

"So?"

He shrugs. "I never pictured you in a fluffy wedding dress."

"But you did picture me in one, just not like this?"

"Theoretically."

Color flames my cheeks. "Well, I'd change, but I have nothing else to put on. Or my phone to call anyone. Or my credit card to order something." I fall back into the cushions, wincing. "I'm sorry I got you into this mess."

He exhales roughly and walks my way. His features are without the playfulness of a few minutes ago. He's serious—sober—and my heart pounds.

Luke stops in front of me with his hands slung in his pockets. The sun kisses his short hair, highlighting how much darker it's gotten since I last saw him. All I want to do is reach for him, have him pull me into his arms, and tell me it'll all be okay.

But I don't.

"I'll tell you what," he says, his voice low and gravelly. "I need to go to the barn for a little bit. I have a few things to do. Why don't you go find something else to wear? We'll talk when I get back, and you aren't dressed like you're getting ready to marry someone else."

"I told you I don't have anything."

He turns before I can read his features and grabs his phone. "Well, you figured out how to break into my house. Pretty sure you can figure out how to break into my closet."

Laughter falls from my lips as he disappears into the kitchen again. The sliding glass door that leads to the back of the house opens and then closes. *That was easy.*

This could've gone so differently. Luke could've been an asshole, and it would've been justified. Maybe our breakup wasn't contentious, but I *am* his ex-girlfriend. Even though I haven't seen a serious girlfriend or a wife on his social media, that doesn't mean one doesn't exist. Without a woman in his life, he still could've been pissed that I waltzed into his house without so much as a hello. Luke could've walked straight out the door after telling me to get out and I couldn't have blamed him.

I grin. *But he didn't.*

He was Luke, the easygoing, good-natured, gold-hearted man who would give you the shirt off his back. Or out of his closet. *It's no wonder I once loved this man.*

The stillness descends upon me again almost immediately. This time, it doesn't feel like it will swallow me whole. Instead, it's almost a gift. It's space for me to get my head together and figure out what to do.

I glance down at the fabric pooling all around me.

"First things first," I say, setting my glass on the table. "Let's get out of this thing."

I head upstairs to Luke's room.

Chapter Four

L uke

"I don't know. Maybe I could stay here?"

My steps fall faster, putting more distance between me and ...
her.

What is she doing here?

Laina Kelley and her bright blue eyes and dirty-blond hair is the
last person I expected to see at all, let alone inside my damn house.

Sweat drips down my back. It has nothing to do with the sun. I
swing open the barn doors with more gusto than necessary and step
inside.

Rarely do I feel unable to manage a situation. Sure, I sometimes
present things to my family with a little extra drama just to keep them
on their toes. It's a good time. But it's not very often that I find myself
in a situation that *actually* scares the shit out of me.

Laina chose to come here. *What the hell?*

"What do I do now?" I ask the empty horse stalls.

My body buzzes with a rush of excitement and a flood of adrenaline. I played it cool—I think I did, anyway. I didn't let her see how

much she caught me off guard. But my ability to be controlled and sufficiently detached whittled away at record speed as she looked up at me with unguarded vulnerability.

She may not be mine anymore, but I'd still kill for this girl. That's a complicated and dangerous place to be.

"I just need to process that she's here," I say, pacing the walkway. "Let's set aside the fact that she broke in without talking to me for years. I'll deal with her lack of boundaries later and how she stormed into my personal space like we were twenty years old again and made herself at home."

A grin tickles my lips. I fight it. I try my hardest to stave it off. But the knowledge that Laina knew she could still come to me when she needed help is the best damn thing I've heard in a long time.

"Deal with that later," I tell myself. "Right now, I gotta get my shit straight and get a plan together before I make a fool out of myself."

I pull a folding chair from against the wall and pop it open. Sitting down, I find my phone and look for Gavin's name.

"Hey, Luke. What's going on?" he asks after two rings.

"I kinda have a situation over here."

"Again?" He sighs. "Dammit, Luke."

"*No.* Stop. It's not like that."

"It never is."

I sigh heavily and look at the ceiling. "I mean it."

"You always do."

Asshole. "Look, I'm calling you because—"

"Because Mallet won't answer," he says.

I start to protest, but that's true. Mallet won't answer. He blocked me after I sent him too many texts late at night because apparently training for a big professional fight is more important than humoring your little brother.

"And Chase might answer," Gavin says, "but he'll make you regret it."

Can't argue that one either.

"You could call Kate," he says. But no one calls Kate with *a situation* unless you want it blown out of proportion and given the most expensive, over-the-top, time-consuming solution known to man. "Even you aren't that desperate."

I suck a breath between my teeth. "I don't know. I might be."

"Good. Call her, then."

"Gavin, stop being a fuckhead. I need your help."

He groans to ensure I don't get comfortable calling him for help. Gavin is unequivocally my best friend, but the guy has weaknesses like everybody. He's a great problem solver and is totally a people person. He just doesn't like to be *my* problem solver or involve himself with *my* people issues.

Tough luck this time, sucker.

"I'm going to give you three guesses as to who is in my house right now," I say, swallowing past the lump in my throat.

"Is this one of those things I'm supposed to get in three guesses, or are you just wasting my time?"

"I could give you fifty guesses, and you still won't get it."

"You're wasting my time. Got it."

I roll my eyes. "When people say you have three guesses, they don't actually mean it. You realize that, right? It's a rhetorical question."

"That's not what rhetorical means."

"Uh, yes, it is. The question is being asked for effect, not for an answer."

He snickers. "Okay, boy genius. Do you realize that the way you phrased it wasn't a question? It's a rhetorical statement, *maybe*. But it is not a rhetorical question because there's no damn question."

I groan, my irritation growing fast and wild.

"All right. I'm done. What's going on this time? Who is in your bedroom?" he asks. "And if you say Alyssa after all the shit that went down—"

"It's not Alyssa. I haven't talked to Alyssa in six months."

"Thank God. She's a nice girl and whatever, but the two of you are just not supposed to be together, Luke. We've all tried to tell you. I know you've felt bad breaking things off with her in the past, but I hope for your sake that you mean it when you say you haven't talked to her in six—"

"*Laina Kelley is in my house.*"

The words shoot from my mouth so abruptly, so powerfully, that I flinch.

"Stop playing with me, Luke, you prick. I have shit to do today."

"I'm not kidding, Gav."

"*She got married today.* Everyone in the world knows that. Even I'm not dense enough to believe that one. Now, do you have anything you actually want to say? Or can I go back to texting Tabitha a sob story that I'm making on the fly because I don't want to bartend tonight, but I'm also incapable of telling her *no?*"

I work my neck back and forth. Somehow, sharing this with Gavin—even though he's being a dick about it—relieves some of the energy bubbling in my stomach.

"Luke?"

"Have you checked the news in the last hour or so? I mean, I haven't, but I imagine you won't be able to turn on the television or go online without seeing a headline about Laina Kelley being a runaway bride."

He pauses. The sound changes like he's put me on speakerphone. Another few beats pass before he gasps. "*You're shitting me.*"

"Believe it or not, this is one thing I wouldn't joke about."

"Okay, let me get this straight. Laina came all the way from Los Angeles with half of Hollywood in tow to get married to the biggest star of our generation. But she bails at the last minute and has gone *missing in action,* according to the media. And somehow, she winds up in *your* house?"

"You got it."

He's silent for a few moments, and I can picture him scrolling through his phone to check the headlines.

"Tell me you didn't do anything to cause this," he says warily.

"Because a ton of shit is floating around online already with all kinds of speculation."

"The fact you think I would break up a wedding is insulting. *But,* the fact that you think I'm capable of convincing Laina not to marry Tom Waverly ..." I'm smug. "Very flattering. Thank you."

The sound bobbles again. This time, the roar of his engine cuts through the line, then ceases before he returns.

"Just got home," he says, a door screeching in the background. "Now, fill me in. What the hell is going on? Have you been talking to her? Have you seen her lately—besides now, obviously? How have you been able to keep this from me?"

I laugh. "I haven't."

"You haven't what?"

"I haven't been talking to her. I haven't seen her. I haven't kept shit from you. Cotton called me this morning to shoe one of his horses. Did that, came home, and found Laina sitting on the couch in her wedding gown."

"What did she say?"

"She hasn't said much, but I haven't pushed her. I asked why she walked out once, and she gave me a deer-in-the-headlights look, so I changed the subject. It's not really important now."

"No, you're right. Is she okay?"

I take a deep breath and try to settle the whisper of anxiety breezing around my insides.

Gavin's question and vague insinuation make sense. After all, he knows her. They were once close, too. Our whole family was close to Laina. She might be fun-loving and spontaneous, but she's not the kind of person to leave her fiancé at the altar. Something big must have happened. I just hope that big event was realizing she wasn't happy and not something ... darker.

My shoulders tense as I push the thought out of my mind. For now.

"She seems fine," I say, running a hand through my hair. "A little frazzled. But, you know, if she wasn't sitting in this giant wedding dress, it could've easily just been a normal afternoon." I laugh at the bizarreness of it all. "Well, as normal as finding your ex-girlfriend who's now a huge pop star in your house on her wedding day."

I pace again, unable to stand still.

"Hey, Luke. Are *you* okay?"

"Of course, I'm fine. Why wouldn't I be?"

Gavin's voice lowers. "Because the one who got away is suddenly back, and I know you weren't expecting it."

I sigh and stop moving, my heart pounding. I'm not sure what to say. He'll know I'm lying if I try to say it's no big deal. But how do I answer that?

Laina is, without a doubt, the love of my fucking life.

She's unlike any woman I've met—a perfect ten in every way. She's gorgeous and beautiful, talented and hilarious. Sweet but a spitfire. Predictable yet mischievous. Laina is headstrong and determined, too, but none of those qualities are what I love most about her.

What makes it impossible to move on from her completely is that *I like her.*

I like her as a person. I respect the hell out of her. I enjoy being with her, even when we aren't having sex—maybe even more when we aren't in the bedroom.

That's great when she's your girl, but it's not so great when she's not, and you can't have her.

Like now.

Because she left me for bigger—much-deserved—things. A brighter, bolder life. I don't think Gavin is entirely right. She's not back. She's just here ... for now.

"She needs my help, Gav. I don't know why, but it doesn't matter. If she needs me, I'll be there."

"I know you will, buddy."

My smile is faint. "She wants to stay."

"For how long?"

I shrug even though he can't see me.

27

"Look, I have concerns that this isn't safe *for you*," Gavin says.

"I—"

"But I know you're going to help her anyway." He chuckles. "What can I do to help?"

I grin. "Have I ever told you that you're my favorite brother?"

"Yes. But you usually only say it when you need a favor."

"Bad idea to mention it now, then, huh?"

He laughs.

I rack my brain for anything that Gavin might be able to do to help. The only thing I can come up with is that Laina mentioned she doesn't have a phone or clothes. Sure, she can borrow both of mine. But she might feel more comfortable not being dressed in her ex's clothes while she sorts her life with another man.

"Can you get a prepaid cell phone?" I ask. "She doesn't have hers, and I'm guessing she's going to want to make calls and not have them easily traced."

"Don't ask questions, but I have a prepaid cell that I haven't activated yet. You can have that."

Don't ask questions? Now, all I want to do is ask questions. *What are you up to, Gav?*

"Great," I say instead, staying focused. "And can you grab her a few clothes somewhere?"

"Where do you think I'm going to be able to get women's clothes?"

I run a hand down the side of my face. "Go to Chase's and see if Kennedy will let you borrow a few things. She's a teenager, but I think they're about the same size."

"Oh, sure. How should I ask our niece if I can borrow some of her clothes? She's going to get the wrong impression."

I laugh. "Make something up. Tell her you have a girl over from out of town or something."

"That's not setting a good example."

"Sure. Worry about that now."

"Fine, fine. I'll do it."

"And, Gav, please don't mention this to anyone. I don't want anyone to know Laina is here."

I can almost hear his smile through the phone. "You got it."

"Thanks."

"I'm going to go have a super awkward conversation with Kennedy. Do you want me to bring the stuff over, or are you coming to get it?"

I glance back toward the house. "Can you bring it over?"

"Sure. I'll let you know when I'm on my way."

"Thanks, man."

"No problem."

"Bye."

I end the call and sling my arms over the gate overlooking the field. The sun is warm on my face as I stare at the horizon.

"The most important thing is that I keep my head together," I say, my voice carried off by the wind. "She's not here for me. She's here because she needs me as a friend, and I cannot, no matter what, screw that up."

I pull my arms back and let out a long sigh.

Don't screw this up. That's funny. Screwing up is what I do best.

I pivot on my heel and head back to the house.

Chapter Five

L aina

    "You would think," I say, groaning and stepping out of a pile of white fabric, "that getting out of a wedding dress would be easier than this."

I turn slowly and face the discarded garment.

A heaviness settles in my chest, aching between my breasts. It would be unbearable if there wasn't an even heavier feeling of contentment in my soul. I catch a glimpse in the full-length mirror leaning against the wall—a mirror I bought at a yard sale and put in that exact spot one summer afternoon.

My hair is swept up in the back, with tendrils framing my face. There's enough makeup on my skin to film a movie. My breasts hang freely, and the white thong showcases the spray tan I didn't want to get. I don't *look* like me. No wonder I haven't *felt* like me lately. Everything I always liked about myself—my freckles, sense of humor, boundless energy—is all gone.

I race into the en suite and find a washcloth and towel. Using a new bar of soap from beneath the sink, I scrub my face until my skin is pink. The abrasion of the cloth and sting of the soap are probably as metaphoric as they are cleansing, but when I look in the mirror over the vanity, I'm ... free.

"There you are, Laina," I say, smiling at my reflection. "Nice to see you again."

It takes longer to settle my hair. Thanks to all the product the glam team used to make it picture-perfect and more bobby pins than was necessary, it takes my fingers and a comb I locate in a drawer to get it in some semblance of normalcy. I find a rubber band and pull it into a ponytail.

Each layer I peel away removes a cloak I knew was uncomfortable but didn't realize how suffocating it was until now.

Tom won't come in and see me without makeup and make a snide comment. He won't mention that I won't fit into my wedding dress if I don't get my ass to the gym this morning. There is no chance he'll come through the door and find a way to work a lyric from one of my songs into the conversation just so he can tease me about the *juvenile language* or *ridiculous themes* of my music.

And the look in his eyes, an arrogance that twinkled just enough to make me nervous, will no longer make my stomach tighten when we inevitably argue about one of those things.

"You're good," I whisper to myself. "This is not a dream."

I wash the soles of my feet and dispose of the cloth in the bottom of the shower. *I'll get that later.* Then I make my way to Luke's closet.

"Okay, we have a shirt from the feed store, one from a power tools company, another from the feed store." I laugh, sorting through the bin of shirts on the floor. "Oh, here's a purple one from the feed store. Bet this was an exclusive piece of merch."

I snort and pull the shirt over my head. The air is filled with the scent of his cologne—a warm pepperiness with a hint of apple, and the smell of his mother's laundry detergent. The combination makes me smile from ear to ear.

Discarding my thong into the mass of tulle, the last layer of the morning to go, I throw on a pair of his boxers.

Then I breathe. Deeply. Completely. Unencumbered.

"Gosh, that feels good," I say, closing the closet.

I turn to figure out what to do with my dress when a cordless phone catches my eye.

"He still has a landline?" I pick it up off the bedside table and press the green button. A dial tone buzzes back at me. "I didn't know people still used these."

I sit on the edge of the bed and wonder if I should go find Luke. But as my gaze travels to the heap of hoops on the floor, I punch Stephanie's number into the phone instead. Surprisingly, she answers.

"Hello?" she asks, her voice full of hesitation.

"Hey, Steph. It's me."

"*Oh, thank God,*" she says, exhaling. "Are you okay?"

I glance around Luke's bedroom. "I'm fine. How are *you*?"

"First, please remind your security team that I am your best friend, and rules don't apply to me. The only reason I didn't commit murder today is because Troy is freaking gorgeous, and I'm hoping he and I can hook up at some point."

My laughter breaks the rest of the tension in my chest. "I'll be sure to do that."

"Otherwise, I'm fine. I'll admit, I did get entirely too much joy out of telling your dad that you weren't going to show up. *And,* I'll also admit that I followed your father into the groom's room to listen to him tell Tom."

I gasp. "*My father told Tom?*"

"He sure did. A couple of security guys trailed us because your father literally started screaming at me and that got their attention."

"I'm so sorry, Steph."

"Don't be." She snorts. "I know he's your dad, so with all due respect, fuck that guy. This literally made my year."

I fall back into Luke's pillows and close my eyes. Imagining my father screaming at Stephanie over something I did makes my stomach heave. But I talk myself down with reminders of how much my best friend dislikes Dad.

As if she knows I need the reminder, she launches into a spiel I hear at least four times a year.

"He doesn't listen to you," she says. "You get no time off. You've been burned out for two years, Laina, and he works you to the bone. He may be your father, but he doesn't have your best interests at heart. If he did, he would've put a stop to Tom Waverly a long damn time ago."

"I don't need someone to put a stop to anything. I'm a big girl."

"Yes, you are. But you're hiding from Tom right now for a reason." She steadies her tone, working to reduce the anger teeming from each word. "I don't know what has gone on because you won't tell me, but I see the way he looks at you when you don't follow his script. If I were a betting girl, I'd say you wanted to get out of this a lot earlier than now but were afraid. Today, you just so happened to be surrounded by security in a place you felt comfortable and at a time when it was do or die. And you chose not to die—thank God."

My heart races. *How did she know?*

"Speaking of a place you feel comfortable," she says, "where are you?"

I sink deeper into the pillows.

I couldn't have had this conversation before today. There was never any privacy. Stephanie and my agent, Anjelica, are the only two people I truly trust, but I never trusted that we weren't being spied on or listened to. Because *everyone* is willing to do Tom Waverly's bidding. It's a part of the charisma that makes him a box-office star.

"Troy brought me to Luke Marshall's house," I say.

"Wait a minute. Luke Marshall ..." She hums. "The hot farrier we stalk on Social?"

"That would be the one."

I can hear her wheels turning. "How do you know him?"

"Luke and I dated for a long time. We met when we were fifteen and started dating at seventeen."

"*You dated the farrier?* Why am I just finding this out? I have literally sat beside you and drooled over this man's social media posts, *and you dated the guy?*"

"Pretty much." I wince.

"How? For how long? Why have I never met him?"

I sit up and prop myself against the leather headboard. "We dated from the time we were seventeen until I came to Nashville. It was just a few weeks before my twenty-fourth birthday. Then we ... I don't know, tried to make it work, kind of. For a couple of years, we talked off and on, and I'd come back to see him every chance I got." A lump settles in my throat. "Then things really took off, and I couldn't come back anymore, and he never came to see me. Things just kind of ended."

My heart burns at the memories, making the cracks from my heartbreak obvious. The worst part of my life coincided with the best time of my career. Balancing the devastation of losing the man who I loved with every piece of me with the exhilaration of my first world tour was the hardest thing I've ever done.

It was harder than walking out of the church today.

"And you are at his house now?" she asks, a hint of mischief in her voice.

"Stop it."

"*What?*"

"I hear the little smirk in your voice," I say. "This was unplanned. I haven't spoken to Luke in years."

"But you sure as hell have been keeping an eye on him."

"Yes, but ..." I pause, working through a thought. "You don't think this makes me a bad person, do you?"

She laughs. "Why would I think that?"

I shift around and can't get comfortable. The bedding is cozy. It's my conscience that's not.

"I was supposed to marry another man today," I say, my voice growing louder. "And now I'm sitting in my ex-boyfriend's house." *Not to mention in his clothes and bed, but details schmetails.*

"You saved yourself from a bad situation and ran to a place you obviously feel safe. That's supposed to make you a bad person?"

Yes. I feel safe here.

The flood of emotions that hit me nearly knock me over. *I feel safe here—the first place I've felt safe in years.*

"Sure, you could've done it differently," she says. "But would it have made you a better person to have gone through with it then publicly divorced later? Is your mental health worth having the world think you're a *good person?*"

"No."

"Exactly."

"And if you feel too guilty, let me remind you that Tom has put you in some prickly situations, too. He asked you to be his wife at the only concert of yours that he's ever attended in the lead-up to his biggest blockbuster of all time—the one that they were pulling no punches to market."

What a nightmare. There was no conversation after his proposal, no chance to get my bearings. We were being watched by twenty thousand people and endless cameras. All I could do was play the part and say yes.

"He could've chosen another week to have those pictures of him leaked—the term used loosely because you know damn good and well that he was behind that. Instead, he chose the week you were on the cover of *Timeless* magazine so he could steal your moment. He hated that you were chosen as Prettiest Person in the World and got more attention than he did."

I squeeze my eyes shut ... because down deep, I know she's right.

"He could've supported your career just like you supported his," she says. "And please don't forget the rumors about Tom in Paris six months ago."

Multiple women. A penthouse. Pictures that he swears were doctored were splashed across covers of all the rag magazines.

My jaw sets.

And my father made excuses for him. Looking back, I numbed myself to the situation—dove harder into work and chose not to pay attention. Survival at its very best. But the true betrayal from the Paris situation wasn't from Tom. It was from my dad.

How could Dad continue to push me to marry Tom? Why did he get me to try to smooth over Tom's abhorrent behavior? Why didn't he see the red flags waving in the sky or, if he did—and I think he did— why did he blow them off?

"You're right," I say. "I did what I had to do."

"That's my girl."

I laugh. "I guess I need to call Anjelica. My PR is through my label, and I'm sure she has questions."

"Fine. But don't think this conversation about Farrier Boy is over." She laughs, too. "In all seriousness, do you need anything? Want anything? What can I do to support you?"

My heart warms. "Just having you to call is the best thing in the world."

"I am pretty special, aren't I?" She laughs again. "Okay. Call Anjelica. Can I call you on this number if I need you?"

"Um, you know what? I don't know how long I'll be here. So just let me figure out a few things, and then I'll call you back with details."

"Okay. I have your stuff from the hotel and your phone, by the way. Troy found it and gave it to me." She sighs blissfully. "My flight leaves tomorrow afternoon. If you decide you want this stuff, please let me know."

"I might. I just need to figure out how to get it. I'm sure you're being watched."

"Yeah. Probably. Hell, I might give them something to see if they want to be assholes."

I giggle. "Okay. I'll call you later. Love you."

"Bye."

"Bye."

I end the call, then dial Anjelica's number before I chicken out.

Every ring ups my anxiety. By the third one, I'm not sure she'll answer. I'm mentally reviewing what my voice message will say when she answers breathlessly.

"Anjelica Grace," she says.

"Hey. It's Laina."

Her exhale could move a mountain. "My God, girl. You're making me work for my money today, aren't you?"

"Sorry."

"Don't be. As your agent and your friend, you made the right choice today. I was envisioning a lifetime of press releases to save your skin if you went through with the marriage."

"Really?"

She laughs dryly. "Moving on, we've been holding off on a statement and hoping you'd call. It's in your email."

I don't have a computer. "Can you read it to me?"

She quickly goes through the statement that doesn't say anything but says everything at the same time.

"Love it. Use it. What else?" I ask.

"We are just doing a little damage control. Nothing for you to worry about. All I need from you is to keep your head down for a little while. This will all blow over, but we need to give it some time to cool off. Hopefully, Tom doesn't want to drag it out and keep his name in the headlines. Do you have a place you can stay?"

I glance around. "I think so. I'm working on it."

"Where can I get ahold of you? Your cell is off. I'm assuming you didn't take it so you can't be tracked."

"You're so smart."

"This isn't my first rodeo." She laughs. "Get a phone and call me with the number in case I need to reach you. Your father has been blowing me up to see if you've checked in. I take it you're avoiding him?"

I huff. "Yes. I can't deal with him right now. He's going to be pissed and try to get me back with Tom because Tom got him in on that golf course deal in San Diego."

"Got ya. I'll tell him you're safe, and that's all he's getting for now. Sound good?"

"Perfect."

"I hope you don't mind, but I checked in with your security team when news broke this afternoon," she says. "It's not my place, and if I overstepped, I apologize. I wanted to know you were safe."

I smile. "That's fine. Thank you for caring."

"Of course. I will let you know that Landry Security is keeping two men in town just in case you need them. They asked me to tell you that if we talked. Apparently, they know where you are and are giving you space, but they're close by."

I can't stop the sniffle. The bridge of my nose burns nearly as hot as my chest. Knowing that these people care about me, even if they are on my payroll, means a whole heck of a lot—especially right now.

"We have your back, Laina. The Mason Music team is battling for you right now. Coy heard the news and called me right away to make sure we were doing everything we can to protect you. Everyone but Boone," she says, her voice rising. "*Get out of my candy jar. I mean it.*"

I snort, imagining Boone Mason driving Anjelica crazy per usual.

The Mason Music staff is nothing short of amazing. They feel closer than business associates to me much of the time. Even the CEO, Coy Mason, and his brother, Boone, reach out personally from time to time. Choosing to work with Anjelica was the best decision I've made in my career.

"Thank you, Anjelica. I appreciate you so much."

"That's what I'm here for. Now go and try to get some rest."

At the mention of sleep, a yawn slips past my lips. I stretch over my head and enjoy the pull through my back.

"Don't forget to call me," she says. "I have to go. Talk soon."

"Goodbye."

I end the call and place the receiver on the bedside table. My dress is still on the floor, and the washcloth is still in the shower. *But this bed is so soft.*

I lie back, intending to close my eyes for a few minutes. The next thing I know, I'm drifting off into a peaceful slumber.

Chapter Six

Laina

A voice inside my head tells me to wake up. It grows louder, working its way into my dream until I finally crack open my eyes.

Where the heck am I?

Pale yellow walls. A navy comforter covering my legs. A television too big to be practical mounted on the wall across from the bed.

Luke's.

My cheek is stuck to the pillowcase by my slobber as I try to sit up. The day's events come rolling through my mind, ruining the beautiful moments of post-slumber bliss. A twinge of a headache licks behind my temple.

What time is it?

The sky outside the window is orange and purple. Luke's house is completely still. A clock on the bedside table reads mid-evening. I've been asleep for *three hours.*

I spring to my feet and step over my dress, working to regather my hair into the rubber band. The strands are smashed against the side of my head from where I slept on them. Without a mirror, I can tell that the top is a rat's nest of epic proportions. I should make a pit stop in the bathroom and get myself put together, but my feet march through the hallway and down the half flight of stairs to find Luke.

"There you are," he says, leaning against a kitchen cabinet. "I thought you might sleep all night."

I yawn, my shoulders drooping. "I didn't realize how tired I was."

His gaze draws the length of my body. His lips twitch as his gaze finds mine once again. "I see you found your way through my closet."

"Do you know how many feed store shirts you own?"

He shrugs.

"All of them," I say.

"I like the way they fit."

"Do you ever shop at a store that doesn't sell farm supplies?" I ask.

"Why would I do that?" He laughs at my expression. "You have a little something on your cheek."

I wipe at the spot he motions toward and find a sticky blob that must be snot. My face heats so hot that it's warm to the touch.

"It happens to the best of us," he says as I wipe my hand on a paper towel, then move to the sink. "Did you sleep okay?"

"Apparently. I lie down for a minute, and it's three hours later." I finish washing my hands. "I used your landline to make a couple of calls. I hope that's okay."

"Of course."

We stand close enough to touch if our weight shifts just enough. My skin tingles at the proximity. I tell myself it's because I need comfort and not because of anything else—surely not because I'm still attracted to Luke.

His half smile, like he can read my mind, gets me every time.

I turn off the tap. "My friend Stephanie and agent, Anjelica, seem to have taken care of everything."

"That's good." He stretches his legs out in front of him. "You haven't talked to Tom?"

"No. That's a big no."

He nods, following me with his eyes as I take a dish towel from the drawer.

"I'll probably never talk to Tom again," I say, drying my hands. "Is that weird?"

I shrug. "I suppose it's weird if you're on the outside. You probably think it's odd that I could've been marrying a man this morning, yet I'll never talk to him again now." I hold the towel in my hands and look at Luke. "But it's really a relief."

So many words are on the tip of my tongue, but I don't have the guts to say them. It's for the best that I don't anyway. He'll think I'm just overly emotional—and maybe I am. And I'll regret saying them when I return to my life, and he never talks to me again—which he won't.

The best way to predict the future is to look at the past. While our storied history is the sweetest part of my life, it's the end I must use when looking into a crystal ball.

Even though as I stand in his kitchen and peer into those bright green eyes, feeling the connection between us reverberate in the air, it's hard to remember why it didn't work out.

"I owe you an explanation," I say, realizing I've never given him a reason for being here.

"You really don't."

"No, but I do." I move across the room to put some distance between us. Only when we're more than a few feet apart can I breathe again. "And I want you to know that it was really brazen of me to *use the key to get in your house*." I return his grin. "And it was even kinder of you to have been as sweet to me as you have."

"Let me ask you this," he says, smirking. "What would you have done if you had broken in here and my wife was in my bed?"

"I would have questions."

"Such as?"

My grin grows. "I would've asked you why you never showed pictures of your wife on social media."

His loud laughter fills the room.

"I mean, I get that you use your page for work, but you could still show her every now and then," I say, laughing too. "I'm always suspicious if a man is married and his girl doesn't show up anywhere with him online."

"*Oh*," he says, his eyes alight with humor. "I see. You've been checking me out."

"Hardly."

He hums.

"Stephanie happened to see one of your viral videos," I say, rolling my eyes playfully. "And she showed me, and I may or may not have gotten curious."

"You're a fangirl."

It's my turn to burst out laughing. "I am hardly a fangirl, Luke. But thanks."

"You are. That is *so* cool."

"Stop it."

"Why? You don't think I'm not online watching what you're up to?"

He turns away before I can see his face.

"You're checking on me?" I ask.

"I just wonder what you're up to sometimes." His voice drops a few octaves. "You're really impressive. But I'm sure you know that."

My heart swells so big that I'm afraid it will burst.

After I was supposed to come home the last time and couldn't, he didn't answer my calls. Worse, he didn't return them, either. I've always hoped that maybe it was too hard for him like it was for me. A clean break was easier than peeling the bandage off slowly. I've looked into endless arenas and at thousands of crowds—read countless comments on posts and wondered if any of them were him.

I've wondered whether Luke thought about me. To have the answer, *to know that he has*, brings tears to my eyes because what I've really feared all these years is that he hated me. *Did he hate me for leaving? Did he hate me for not coming back? Even though he told me he knew I had to go try to achieve my dreams, did he really mean it?*

Knowing that Luke was always in my corner, rooting for me if only silently, heals a wound I've carried with me since the day I left Peachwood Falls.

"The peach dress that you wore to the awards show last spring," he says, looking at me over his shoulder. "It reminded me of the one you wore to senior prom." He dips his chin and looks away again. "I'm sure it was a lot more expensive, and those diamonds were real, but you were beautiful."

My vision fogs as I will myself not to cry.

"Anyway," he says, running a hand over his head. "I'm glad things are okay, and your people are fighting for you behind the scenes."

Like I never fought for you.

Like you never fought for me.

"Yeah," I say, clearing my throat. "They're all in agreement that my stunt this afternoon was the best thing I could've done in the moment."

Luke faces me again. "And you don't think you'll ever talk to Tom again?"

His features are sober, and his brows pull together. The question hangs in the balance between us.

I'm not sure why it seems important to answer this fully—but it does.

"Tom didn't love me, Luke. Not like a man should love a woman if he's going to marry her. And I didn't love him like a woman should love her husband, either."

He stares into my eyes.

"I was convenient for him," I say. "I helped him reach his goals. I bolstered his public persona. But there was little respect there. No fun." I gulp. "No sex."

"*What?*"

I exhale and turn to the sink, watching a horse approach the barn.

"Tom isn't a terrible human being," I say. "He's no saint, but he's not the devil. Mutual friends set us up, and it was great at first. But then I went off on tour, and he went off making movies, and we weren't really around each other all that much. A weekend here, a couple of weeks there."

Luke drags a chair out from the small round table near the sliding glass doors and sits.

"Then Tom asked me to marry him in front of the world, basically, and I couldn't say no. And, before I knew it, a wedding was planned, and I was neck-deep in this whole ... *production.* Then what do you do? Everything is ordered and reserved. The entire planet knows it's happening. I just stuck my head in the sand and worked and tried to block it out." I laugh sadly. "It didn't hit me until this morning that *we would be married.* I would be attached to this man who I barely knew, a man who I hadn't had sex with in six months. A man who if I had to start dating all over again, I would pass. How could I *marry him?*"

"You can't." His voice makes me jump. "For what it's worth, I'm proud of you. It had to be hell to walk out of there today."

I try to reply but fail. I can't speak. All I can do is swim in the depths of his kind eyes.

"Oh, and in case you're wondering," he says, a smile tugging at the corner of his mouth. "If another woman had been here today, I wouldn't have asked you to leave."

"You really don't know how much that means to me," I say softly.

"I told you once that I would always be here for you. I meant it. And you don't know what it means to me that you knew that."

I start to respond, but the sound is hollow. A sob catches in my throat.

"But I am telling you that if someone comes here looking for you, you better tell me so I can get backup," he says, winking. "I'm not as young as I once was."

It's enough to break through my emotions and elicit a laugh. He glances at his phone.

"You're thirty," I say, sniffling.

"It's been a rough thirty years."

He stands and walks to me, grinning. "Come here."

45

I nearly collapse in his arms, burying my head against his shoulder. My arms wrap around his middle, and my knees buckle. But I don't care.

"You're tough," he says, holding me against him. "You're going to get through this and be stronger than you were before. Just hang in there."

I breathe him in, letting his proximity soothe me.

This. When was the last time I was hugged like this? When did I last feel like someone was pouring their strength and care into me? Who was the last person to take me in their arms and make me feel so ... whole?

"Why does it seem possible when you say it?" I ask.

"Because I'm always right."

I giggle. With every move, my cheek brushes against his rock-solid chest.

"Now, I have to tell you something, and I hope you're not mad," he says.

What? I pull away, my heart leaping to life. "What in the heck does that mean?"

"I told Gavin you were here," he says, wincing. "I only told him so he could pick you up a few things. He won't say a word to anyone. I promise."

My jaw drops. "*That's* what you have to tell me, and you hope I'm not mad?" I smack his chest, earning an *ouch* from Luke. "And don't patronize me with that ouch."

He laughs, licking his lips.

"I'd like to see Gavin," I say, thinking about his adorable smile.

"Good. Because he's here."

"He is?"

Luke gives me the sweetest, sexiest grin that melts me to my core. "Come on."

Chapter Seven

L uke

"It's me!" Gavin shouts from the entryway moments before Laina and I come around the corner. "Wow. She really is here."

Laina giggles and runs toward my brother. He thrusts a pizza at me and drops a few bags to the floor just in time to catch Laina in a huge hug.

"Sure. Leave me here holding the pizza," I mumble.

Gavin looks at me over Laina's shoulder and winks.

"My gosh, Gavin," she says, pulling away from him. "It's so good to see you."

"I'm as handsome as ever, right?"

She laughs, her cheeks rosy. "How are you? What have you been up to?"

"Oh, the regular. Working at Steele's Farm during the day and The Wet Whistle some nights for shits and giggles."

"Sounds downright delightful," Laina says. "Are you seeing anyone? Married? Kids?"

"Guess you haven't been following him online," I say under my breath.

She hears me and casts me a smile.

"Me?" Gavin asks. "Hell, no. Kids are a hard limit. I remember what a pain in the ass I was growing up, and I have absolutely no interest in offering the universe a chance to pay me back."

"Fair," she says.

"And no lady friend at the moment. I'm kinda enjoying my freedom."

Laina crosses her arms over her chest. "Trust me. Be careful in relationships because, before you know it, you can be standing in a church about to get married and realize it's the worst thing you could ever do."

Gavin makes a face. "Yeah. That's a hard *no* from me." He bends down and picks up the bags. "I came bearing gifts."

"Ooh, you did?" Laina asks.

"Luke asked me to round up a few things for you, so I worked some magic."

She looks over her shoulder and gives me a soft grin. It hits me square in the heart. *Oof.*

"I have a couple of shirts and shorts, courtesy of Kennedy, who now thinks I have a woman trapped in my house or something." He shakes his head. "I told her she was sick and couldn't go home, and she just kind of smirked at me." He looks at me. "How does she do that?"

"Because she's us, Gav."

He snorts. "Poor Chase. Anyway, I also brought you a prepaid cell phone." He hands a box to Laina. "You'll have to activate it. All the stuff is in this bag. And I also didn't ask for this, but Kennedy sent shampoo and face wash and stuff. Apparently, she thinks I'm a heathen and have no toiletries."

"Do you?" I ask.

"Hell, no."

We all laugh.

It's so nice to stand here with the two of them, talking about stupid shit. Gavin and I see each other just about every day at some point, but it's different tonight.

I take in Laina and observe her interaction with my brother.

Or maybe she's just the difference.

"This was so sweet of you, Gavin," Laina says, grinning at me. "And you, too, Luke."

"Hey, he might've requested this stuff, but I'm the one who did the dirty work," Gavin says. "I even went to town and battled the crowds from the wedding ...." He stops and frowns. "Shit. Sorry."

Laina shakes her head. "It's fine. Don't be sorry."

Gavin doesn't look convinced but moves along anyway. "I got you snacks and juice boxes." He pulls a bundle of cherry-flavored children's drinks from a bag. "Ta-da!"

"I haven't had one of these in forever," she says, taking the package from him. "How did you think of this?"

"That one is all me. You know how you associate people with odd things? Or maybe it's just me that does it," Gavin says.

"No, I do it, too," Laina says.

"Me, too," I say. "I can't think of Mallet and not think of that pink bubble gum that he always chewed. He'd stick it under the table before dinner until Mom caught on and about killed him."

Gavin laughs. "I associate Laina with cherry drinks because that one summer we mixed the hell out of that shit with vodka. Do you guys remember that? We'd get the alcohol, and Laina would get the juice or whatever that stuff actually is."

She catches my eye, and we exchange a look. *How could I forget that summer?* Skinny-dipping at the lake. Driving around for hours with her next to me while listening to classic rock. Getting hamburgers from The Wet Whistle and driving out into one of Cotton's fields to talk until the stars came out.

It was one of the best summers of my life.

"And I brought you guys dinner," he says, nodding toward the pizza in my hand. "I figured you'd had enough for the day and just wanted to relax."

I smile at my brother.

"You are the best, Gavin," Laina says, giving him a quick hug. "Thank you for going out of your way to do all of this."

"That's what friends are for," he says. "Now, I gotta go. In order to keep up this wild ruse, I told Kennedy I was getting ice cream for the sick woman in my house. The little con artist asked for her own pint as payment." He backs toward the door. "You owe me a pint of ice cream, Lucas."

I laugh. "I'm sure you'll swindle more than that out of me."

"I absolutely will." He opens the door. "It was great seeing you, Laina. Maybe I'll see ya around."

"Maybe."

Gavin gives us a half wave, half salute and leaves. The door shuts with a thud.

"He's like a whirlwind," Laina says, picking up the bags. "I can't believe you had him do all of this, and he really did it. That was so nice of you guys."

"I just didn't want you to wear all my clothes."

She jabs me in the ribs with her elbow. "I think it means you're going to let me stay."

My stomach muscles contract from the look in her eye.

It would be so easy to forget that she's here because she's running from her life. If I really wanted to, I could wipe away the fact that she's a famous singer and that she left me once over that. Without trying, I could fall so hard for this woman that I couldn't see straight.

But I can't forget I'm a momentary safe house. I know better than to forget how it killed me when I couldn't see her again—when her world had engulfed her completely. The shift from being a fixture in her life and a certain part of her future to simply becoming a boy from her past knocked me sideways. A part of me has never recovered.

I have to guard myself from falling in love with her all over again because I did that once and barely survived. I don't think I could do it again.

Laina holds the bags at her sides and yawns. "I don't know how I'm still tired after that nap."

"Let's take all this upstairs so you can get a shower later if you want."

"Okay."

I wait for her to go up the steps first and follow her with the pizza box. It's so natural having her in my home. It's so easy spending time with her. *How can it be this simple after all these years? After the heartbreak of my life?*

It probably feels right because I'm only showing her "healed and easygoing Luke" and not the "I hate the world Luke" I was for a long time after we ended.

"Ugh," she says, stutter-stepping in the doorway to my bedroom.

I nearly run the edge of the pizza box into her back. "What's wrong?"

"Nothing. I just left my dress on the floor, and seeing it just felt like ..." She sighs and goes into my bedroom. "It didn't feel good."

I drop the box on the bed. "Let's do something with it, then."

"Like what?"

"I don't know. What do you want to do with it?"

She sets the bags in the bathroom and then returns to the bedroom. She studies the big white poof on the floor.

"We could put it in a trash bag and save it," I offer, not sure what women do with these things. *So much money for one day. Or half a day in this case.*

"I don't want to save it."

"Okay. We could bag it up and donate it to charity."

Her eyes shine. "Let's do that."

I grab a lawn and leaf bag from the kitchen, and we make quick work of stuffing the dress inside. Once the material is out of sight, the relief on Laina's face is evident. Her wrinkled forehead eases. The lines around her mouth soften. Her shoulders slump forward as if a weight has been lifted, and if I had known this would help her, I would've done it hours ago.

I toss the bag into the hallway. "I'll take it to the garage later."

She free-falls backward onto the bed.

My shirt cradles her body, sucking against her front. Her tits sit on top of her chest with the nipples pressing against the fabric, and the hem of my boxers ride up and pool at the apex of her thighs. Her skin is tanned and smooth. She's delicate yet strong, beautiful yet the embodiment of sexy.

My cock twitches in my jeans.

"Do you want to eat or go to sleep?" I ask, moving into the bathroom to adjust myself without her noticing.

"Can I eat in bed?"

"This isn't a hotel."

"No, but I'll be super careful and not drop a crumb."

Hate to tell you, lady, but I wouldn't kick you out of bed for getting crumbs in the sheets.

She yawns in the other room.

"Did Gavin bring you everything you need?" I ask.

"I think so. Thank you again for organizing that for me."

Sufficiently calm, I go back into the bedroom and sit on the other side of the pizza box from her.

"My best friend flies out tomorrow and has all of my stuff," she says. "I'm not sure how to get it from her if you let me stay a few days."

"Just a few days?"

She shrugs, flicking open the pizza box. "Maybe in a few days things will have blown over enough that I can get to the airport and go somewhere else. I don't know where I'll go, but I can figure something out." She sits up and takes a slice of pizza. "Where would you go if you could go anywhere?"

I take a slice, too. "Fuck if I know. Anywhere?"

"Anywhere."

I try not to watch her lips wrap around the edge of the crust. "Montana, maybe."

"You can go anywhere in the world, and you pick Montana?" She laughs. "The world is bigger than the continental US, you know."

"Yeah, well, I'm pretty damn happy here."

"You don't want to see the world?"

"Sure. Peru would be cool. Egypt. Jordan. Iceland," I say, rattling off a few places that might interest me. "But Peachwood Falls has all I need."

She holds my gaze. *Except you. It hasn't had you for the past six years ... and that isn't going to change.*

And it's better that way. At least for me.

I clear my throat and look away. "You know I love it here. I love being with my family. I love living in Poppy's house and working in the business he started when he was my age. Every morning, I wake up and have coffee and look across the fields and feel really lucky. Very ... I don't know. Rooted, maybe. Grounded." I look at her. "This is my home, and I don't really need to travel the world to feel complete. I'd rather have a Sunday dinner with my family than a fancy steak in some restaurant half a world away."

"I miss that."

"What?"

She swallows a bite of her pizza. "I miss that feeling of home. I have five houses across the world. There are two in Nashville—one I just got for an investment. I shared one in Los Angeles with Tom, so I don't know what will happen with that. None of my stuff is really there, so I don't actually care all that much. I have one in New York and one in London."

"*Wow.*"

"But there's not one of them that feels like *home*, you know?"

"I think it's more about the people than the location."

She puts her pizza back in the box and stretches out across my bed. Her eyelids start to get heavy.

"That's probably the problem," she says. "I don't have anyone at any of those places who really cares about me."

My heart pulls so tight I wince. "I doubt that's true."

"It's true." Her eyes close, and her body relaxes into the blankets. "I pay everyone to care. Everyone but Stephanie. But she has her own life."

I sit still and watch her fall asleep. Her breathing evens out. Her lips purse together like they always did. I used to tease her about it and say she was waiting for a kiss even in her sleep. She didn't think I was funny.

I don't think it's anything to laugh about tonight, either.

I close the pizza box and move it to the end of the bed. Then I grab the blanket I covered her with earlier and drape it over her body.

For half a second, I consider climbing into bed with her. I ache to curl up behind her and pull her close. To feel her in my arms. To be reminded of what it's like with her against me.

But then reality hits, and I take the pizza box, turn off the light, and leave her to sleep. This time with Laina isn't about connecting.

It might be our chance to properly say goodbye.

And that's a motherfucker.

Chapter Eight

Laina

Shoes. I still don't have shoes.

I pad down the stairs in one of Kennedy's outfits. The shorts are a bit tight in the ass, and they're a little shorter than I'd choose for everyday wear, and the shirt definitely makes my boobs look a cup bigger. *No complaints there.* I'm still without shoes, underwear, and a bra. One way or the other, I will have to resolve this today.

The house is bright as I round the corner to the kitchen. The coffee pot is half full, and I quickly pour myself a big mug. After a tremendous night's sleep and a scalding hot shower, I finally feel refreshed and ready to take on the day.

Mostly. I've avoided the television for the two percent part of me that's not quite ready to see all the shitty tabloid headlines. It's always a good time to see your name smeared across magazines and online articles using evidence from *confidential sources* to back their theories.

I can only begin to wonder what *confidential sources* shared about me yesterday. I imagine it's the wildest of the wild, yet I bet I'll still be surprised. They never cease to amaze me with their story-telling abilities. *But the thing is ...* I grin. *I don't care.* I don't want to feed the flames or engage with the stories, but I don't feel a burgeoning responsibility to get ahead of it.

"This feels *amazing*," I say, bouncing with energy. "This feels like ... *me*."

I can breathe this morning. There isn't a pebble between my breasts waiting for an opportunity to turn into a stone. My stomach isn't churning, and the acid pit that usually resides there has drained. I'm not waiting for another shoe to drop.

Is this what it feels like to be alive?

I take a sip of my coffee and revel in the morning sun. It never occurred to me how much I worried about publicity and fretted over my public persona *because of Tom.*

Before our relationship, I didn't worry too much about the media. Stories came out and were fabricated to fit a narrative, but they never really mattered. Chatter would come and go—usually about an untrue budding relationship—but my fans never took any of it seriously. And none of it bothered me.

Until I started dating him.

Tom's obsession with his reputation was off the charts. I had to watch what I said in interviews and be careful being photographed in public. He hired his publicist to work with me to master handling questions involving him—and painting *him* in a good light. They were masterful in their setup, presenting their arguments as good for our relationship. *As good for me.* They sold it so well. But our tandem effort undoubtedly made his stock go up while, in retrospect, it took away my personality and the quirks that make me relatable.

My concern for Tom's reputation stifled mine. It's a pattern I increasingly recognize as I think about it. *Tom's wins for the sake of my losses.*

I gaze out the kitchen window. The barn doors are open, and Luke's truck is backed up to the front of it. It's still so early—for me, anyway—and the man is already working hard.

"Why is that so sexy?" I ask before taking another sip of my coffee.

There's something hot about a man working with his hands. Those types of men are strong and capable and can manhandle you in all the right ways. I take another drink, and Luke emerges from the barn and throws something into the back of his truck. He disappears back inside the barn.

I wonder what manhandling capabilities he has these days.

Heat ripples through my body. The urge to be close to Luke burns through me like a hot match.

My first instinct is to fight it—to turn away and distract myself elsewhere. But then I remember I'm no longer attached to Tom. *And I never felt this around him.*

I recall how exciting it was early in our relationship to be with the Hollywood heartthrob. He was so handsome and could be utterly charming. As time wore on, that side of him became less visible privately until the end, when it was mostly nonexistent. Even at the peak of attraction, I never looked at him and felt like *this*.

"I forgot what this even felt like," I say, opening the door and stepping out onto the porch.

Birds sing from the trees overhead, and their melodies float through the breeze like a cheerful soundtrack from nature. I walk along the driveway, through the cool, damp lawn, and to the barn. Luke comes into view as I grow close. He stops, shoving his hands in his front pockets, and leans against his truck.

My God.

A baseball hat sits backward on his head. It's blue, bringing out the blue in his flannel. The denim encasing his muscular thighs is dark. *And his boots? Damn.*

"Morning," he says, smiling. "How did you sleep?"

"Like a log."

He laughs. "I heard you snoring from the couch."

"*You did not.*" I jab him with my elbow and try not to recoil from the contact. "Did you really sleep on the couch?"

"Yeah. You didn't find me in bed with you, did you?"

I worry my bottom lip between my teeth. *No, I didn't.* I thought maybe he got up before I did even though it didn't appear anyone had slept beside me. If he didn't ... *why?*

"You should've woken me up and made me go to the couch," I say.

"If you stay much longer, I might do that. My back hurts like hell today."

I frown.

"I'm kidding," he says, grinning. "My back does hurt, but I don't know if I could make you sleep on the couch. It feels rude."

"It would be rude."

He shakes his head.

"You know what else is rude?" I tease.

"What's that?"

"I woke up, and there was no breakfast ready."

He snorts and heads back into the barn. "This isn't a bed-and-breakfast, Pumpkin."

My cheeks already ache from smiling. "What are we doing today?"

"I'm going to Cotton's to shoe a couple of horses."

"On a Sunday?"

"*Yes, on a Sunday,*" he says, mocking me. "Horses don't give a damn what day it is."

"Oh. You're just going to leave me here?"

He throws a bag over his shoulders and heads back to the truck. "Are you going to get all nervous about being in my house alone *now?* It's a little late for that."

"Very funny." I follow him through the barn. "How long will it take?"

"A few hours, probably. We have one horse out there with founder. I gotta meet with the vet and see what he recommends shoe-wise."

"Sounds complicated."

Luke leans against the truck and crosses his arms over his chest. "What are you going to do today?"

I take a sip of my coffee to avoid a quick response.

I had planned on spending the day with him, but I'm not certain what I thought we would do—nothing and everything, maybe. The news that he won't be here startles me a bit, and it throws me off my game.

"Well, Stephanie leaves Indiana this afternoon, so I might try to figure out how to get my stuff from her without tipping anyone off," I say finally.

"If she wants to leave it at The Wet Whistle, I can swing by after I leave Cotton's."

"Okay."

"Or you could set up a rendezvous with Gavin." Luke laughs. "He could meet her at the coffee shop in Brickfield so she doesn't have to come all the way to Peachwood Falls. Believe it or not, Gavin can be pretty slick."

I laugh, too. "Well, he did put a sticky note on the phone box with his number on it."

"Really?"

The question's simple, but the tone doesn't sound so easy.

"Now I have his phone number, not yours," I say. "I guess if something happens, Gavin will have to be my hero."

"You don't remember my number?"

My cheeks flush, matching the color of Kennedy's shirt I'm wearing. I don't have to answer him. He knows I do.

"Do you need anything from town?" he asks, moving to the driver's door.

I stare at him, curious. *He's really just going to go to work and leave me here?*

It's not that I expect him to stop his life for me, the disruption he didn't necessarily want. But I thought, or maybe just hoped, he would want to catch up a little. And maybe he'd want to stick around to ensure no one inadvertently shows up.

But I guess not.

Maybe I'm wrong about all of this. Maybe he's just too nice to make me leave. *What if he doesn't want me to stay?* I cringe. *Of course, he probably doesn't want you to stay. He has his own life going, and I just plopped in the middle of it.*

I take a shaky breath. "No, I don't need anything from town. Thank you, though." My throat is dry, making the words hard to get out. "By the way, when I talk to Stephanie, I'm going to have her make some calls for me so I can get out of your hair."

Luke squares his shoulders to mine. A flicker of irritation and impatience shines in his eyes.

"Where the hell are you going to go?" he asks, his brows pulled together.

"I'll pick a house and make sure security is there, and it'll be fine."

"Will it, though?"

"Sure," I say, hoping he believes my nonchalant tone. "I can't just stay here indefinitely. Like you said yesterday, I'll cramp your style."

"Like you said yesterday, I don't have a style."

"I woke up this morning and felt guilty for imposing on you like this. I—"

"*Laina.*" He steps to me, cutting the distance between us in half. "Stop talking."

Nerves flutter in the pit of my stomach. I'm torn between falling into his arms and stepping back so I don't do something ridiculous *like fall into his arms.*

My lips part as I drag in quick breaths. Goose bumps prickle my skin. Luke stands in front of me, peering down at my face.

"Stay here," he says.

What?

He looks over my head, running a hand down his jaw. "Nothing will happen to you here. I can guarantee that." His gaze drops to mine again. "Even if someone discovered you were here, I don't have a neighbor that's gonna allow anyone to trespass on their property, and I'll be damned if they get on mine. You can walk around outside. Nap. I mean, think of all the drawers you haven't gone through yet."

A smile pulls my mouth higher.

"Stay here a few days," he says. "See what happens. I'd really like you to stick around."

"Really?"

He leans forward, his eyes twinkling. "*Yes, really.*"

"Okay," I say, trying not to squeal. "But if it goes too long, I'll pay you rent."

"Oh, you're going to pay."

"Excuse me?"

He moseys back to his truck and opens his door. His swagger tells me he's about to screw with me. It's the smirk that guarantees it.

Luke grips the top of the truck with one hand and leans against it. "In exchange for your room and board, you'll help me in the barn."

I blink once. Then twice.

"I'll give you today off since yesterday was a shit show," he says. "But starting tomorrow, your little ass will be out here with me."

My laughter is more disbelief than humor. "Um, hey, Luke. Did you know I'm a singer—a very popular one, at that. *A rich one at that.*"

He chuckles. "I don't give a shit."

"I have money. Lots of it. I'll pay you. In dollars, even."

"I'll see you out here bright and early."

Is he joking? My hand goes to my hip. "You can't ask me to stay and then demand I work. That's illegal, I'm pretty sure."

"While you're going through my stuff today, try to find a pair of sweatpants or something that'll fit you. Kennedy's shorts won't cut it out here."

"Luke, *I am not working in the barn.*"

He winks and climbs into the truck. "You should find yourself a hat, too."

"Luke ..."

The engine roars to life, and he closes his door.

"I hate you," I shout, hoping he can hear me through the glass.

He rolls the windows down and smiles. "Now you get the couch, too."

"Luke!"

But my yelling is pointless because he's already pulling away, his laughter barely heard over the exhaust.

I'd love to kick the gravel like I see angry people do in movies. It looks so spectacular when they do it. Me? Not so much. *Especially without shoes.*

And I'm not *really* angry. I'm not even a little mad. It's hard to be in a bad mood when Luke is so playful.

I look over my shoulder. *Unless he really thinks I'm going to work in that barn. Ick.*

Chapter Nine

L uke

"Hey, Troy, it's Luke. I'm pulling out of the driveway."

I take a left onto the gravel road in front of my house, my gaze lingering on my house through the trees.

"I see you," Troy says from his SUV backed into the woods. "Are you expecting anyone to come by today?"

"The only person who might swing by, although I don't expect him to, is my brother Gavin. Chase, one of my other brothers, is working out of town, and my parents are probably at church. Since Chase is gone, they'll go to lunch with their friends, I bet."

"Gavin drove the black truck last night, correct?"

"Yes. Oh. She's trying to get her stuff here from Stephanie. I don't know what that will entail."

"All right," Troy says. "I'm in communication with Stephanie, so that'll be fine. I'll call you if I need anything."

"Not a problem."

The line goes dead.

I turn away from the highway and take the back roads to Cotton's.

I don't love the idea of leaving Laina at home with Troy lurking in the shadows. As a matter of fact, when he and I came face-to-face this morning by the barn, I almost didn't love it so much that I nearly punched him.

Although, he's one hard motherfucker. I'd rather not tangle with him if I don't have to.

It took him a solid hour to convince me he was part of Laina's security team. He went as far as to have me call a number I found for her agent where a woman named Anjelica confirmed that Troy was legit. Troy and I worked out a way to keep Laina safe while she's here —and he agreed that her being at my house was the best spot for her right now.

No one knows she's here.

Troy is the only reason I'm giving Laina a bit of space today. I know he's there to protect her.

The farther I get away from home, the more I just want to go back. Something must be wrong with me if Laina is there and I'm choosing to go to work. *How many times have I wished for this very scenario? What have I tried to barter with God to get her back?* Now I have her, if only for a limited time, and I'm driving away.

"You have to," I tell myself.

Even if years have passed and Laina isn't the same girl I fell in love with, I still like her. A lot. My heart still knows her. And I can only imagine that the more time we spend together, the harder it will be when she goes.

Holding her in my arms yesterday is now a core memory. If I let my guard completely down—*no.*

I can't let my guard down. I can't keep her. I know that from experience.

She's not mine to keep.

Letting her go comes with the territory. And that part sucks.

I cross Peachwood Creek and pull into Cotton's farm. He waves at me as he climbs out of his truck. I pull up to the stable and turn the engine off.

"I was wondering if you were coming today," he says, shutting the door.

"Sorry." I hop out of the truck. "Got a bit of a late start."

"It's not a problem. I got a bit of a late start today myself. The wife had me hauling stuff from the basement to the trash. Ain't a day goes by that she doesn't have a honey-do list waiting for me in the morning."

"Could be worse," I say, getting my things in order.

"Yeah, I reckon it could. I could be like that sorry son of a bitch who got left standing with his tail between his legs."

My insides twist. "What are you talking about?"

"Oh, you know that bullshit wedding they had going on in Brickfield. Brought half of California with 'em. I ain't been able to get a damn thing done over there in a week. But now it's over, and we can go back to normal." He takes a bag of tobacco out of the front pocket of his overalls. "Surely, you heard about that mess."

I heard about it all right.

My jaw sets, and I head toward the stalls my grandfather worked in as a farrier and his father before him. The nostalgia I usually enjoy here is overrun with Cotton's gossip.

"Do you mind if I do Moe first?" I ask.

"That's fine." He spits in the dirt. "You oughta take a lesson from this fiasco."

I give Moe a scratch before leading her to the clean, dry spot Cotton prepared for us. He stands in the doorway instead of returning to the house like usual. *Great. Just my luck.*

"What kind of a lesson?" I ask, getting the horse and myself situated.

"Well, you're still young and ain't got married yet. Take a look at how that panned out."

I grimace and get to work, running my hand down Moe's leg. She picks up her foot. I start removing her old shoe.

65

"I'm good," I say a little louder than necessary. "There's no wedding on the horizon for me."

"Ah, it's more than that, kid. It's how you pick a wife or a companion if ya ain't getting married. You gotta be smart about it. Find someone tough. The world is a nasty place these days. You better find you a woman who can stand by you through it all."

My heart pumps at Cotton's insinuations—that Laina is weak for not going through with the marriage. *You're at work, Luke. He's just an old man. He doesn't mean anything by it.*

He chuckles.

Fuck it. "What are you saying, Cotton? Spit it out."

"I'm not saying nothin', Luke. Just trying to give you some advice."

I bite my tongue and focus on Moe. Cotton takes a call outside the stable.

Moe's shoe comes off fairly easily, and I get to work cleaning her hoof. Thankfully, she's not too much of a mess. She's calmed down a lot in her old days, making her my favorite—and she knows it.

"You're a good girl, Moe. You're officially the only thing that's cooperated with me in the past few days." I glance up at her big brown eyes. "Well, you and Gavin." I make a face at her, then get back to work. "The world might be ending, come to think of it."

"That new kid I just hired already called in sick for tomorrow," Cotton says, ambling back inside. "How in the hell do people pay their bills when they won't show up for work?"

"Beats me."

He chuckles. "Of course, you don't know. You have the work ethic of your granddaddy."

I keep my head down but nod in appreciation of the compliment. I'm still too pissed about his earlier advice to play too nice.

"Did you ever know your grandmomma?" Cotton asks.

"No. She died the year Mallet was born, I think."

"That's a shame. She was one hell of a woman."

I wipe my brow with the back of my hand. "I've only heard good things about her. But people don't generally tell you all the shitty things someone does once they're gone."

"I'll tell ya." He spits again. "Your grandaddy went to the grave owing me fifty bucks from a poker game."

I snort without looking up.

"It was late one night," he says. "A bunch of us were up at The Wet Whistle trying to stay out of trouble, and someone decided a poker game was the ticket. That was back when you could have alcohol wherever you wanted because the feds weren't sticking their nose into everything like they are now."

"Yeah, you can't do that now." I fit a new shoe onto Moe's hoof. "Unless you're in a casino, I don't even think you can drink and play poker in the same place."

"The world has gone to hell."

I chuckle.

"Anyway, your grandaddy borrowed fifty bucks from me on the last hand and lost his ass." Cotton's belly jiggles as he laughs. "I never let him live it down."

"Want me to pay you back?"

"Hell, no. I shoved another fifty in his casket just so he'll owe me double when I see him next."

I shake my head, not sure what sense that makes. But whatever.

"You look like him, you know that?" Cotton asks. "If I didn't know better, I'd think you were your grandaddy workin' on that horse."

Why are you doing this today?

"Listen to me," he says, chuckling again. "I'm getting old and soft."

"It happens to the best of them."

"That it does."

I sense his proximity growing closer. I finish Moe's shoe and look up. Cotton stands with his hands on his hips, a wad of chew in his lip, staring at me.

"You know, Cotton," I say, stretching my back. "I appreciate all of this ... conversation, but you're starting to freak me out a little bit."

His features fall, and I feel like a dick.

"I've had a hell of a weekend, buddy," I say, moving to Moe's other side. "I'm sorry if I'm being an asshole."

"You're not. I'm freaking me out a little bit, too. Found out yesterday that I have the cancer."

I whip around to face him. "You have cancer?"

"Of the throat." He spits. "Probably from this here tobacco."

"Why don't you stop?"

"It's gonna kill me now anyway. Might as well enjoy it till I'm gone."

I clamp a hand around the back of my neck. *What the heck?*

I don't know what to say to this old man I've known my entire life. *Do I express condolences and make it weird? Do I blow it off like he seems to be doing? Do I ask questions? But what if he doesn't want to talk?*

My chest aches for Cotton, and my thoughts go immediately to his wife, Emma Jo. *That poor woman.* And their only daughter, Traci, must be heartbroken.

"Guess I could've said this an easier way," he says, watching me with steely eyes. "But Emma and I are going to stay with our daughter in Chicago until ... well until I die, I suppose. Traci wants us there with her, and I want the girls together when I go, too. It'll be easier on them."

"Damn, Cotton. I don't know what to say."

"Ain't nothin' to say. We all gotta go at some point. At least I know it's coming and can make it as easy on everyone as I can. It's a blessing, really."

My head spins. *He's dying, yet it's a blessing? How? I don't understand.*

"What do you need?" I ask earnestly. "Let me do something to help. I know Gavin and Chase will be willing to pitch in, too."

He strolls around the stable, watching the ground as he thinks.

My heart hurts as I imagine what he's going through—and not just for himself, although that's scary enough. I bet the heaviest things on his mind are Emma Jo and Traci.

Finally, Cotton stops next to his favorite horse and gives her a nuzzle.

"I didn't have a son, Luke. But if I get one in the next lifetime, I hope he's a lot like you." He grins. "A little less hardheaded and maybe a bit more punctual ..."

I swallow a lump in my throat.

"The only thing you can do for me, kid, is to live a good life. Learn that lesson I was talkin' about earlier."

Although I fought against it earlier, I ask to hear it now. If it's Cotton's last wish for me to listen to his advice, I want to do it for him. That doesn't mean I have to abide by it.

"What lesson?" I ask.

"You got a good heart on ya. You're a hell of a farrier and black-smith, and you're an even better man. Your parents did a damn good job with you."

I sniffle, wiping my nose on my shirt sleeve. *Damn old man.*

"I'm facing certain death. Maybe not today, maybe not tomorrow, but it's coming for me," he says. "And when you get to my age, Luke, and you take stock of all your accomplishments ..."

He sweeps his arms around the stable at the plethora of awards nailed to the walls.

"None of that means anything," he says, dropping his arms. "What matters is the woman in the house and the other in Chicago. That's it. It doesn't get any simpler than that."

I nod warily.

"Make sure you're not just putting work in at the stables," he says. "Put it in where it matters, too."

"I will."

"Nah, kid, *I mean it*," he says, irritated as if I'm blowing him off. "Take a lesson from that wedding last weekend."

Let's not go there, Cotton. Let's not ruin this.

"Did you know that girl who ran out on that movie star was from Brickfield?" he asks.

"I did."

"I didn't realize that. Guess I don't pay enough attention to those things. Emma Jo says I'm the only one who didn't know that."

"Seems about right," I say.

"Get you a girl like that."

What? My head turns to him so fast that my neck pops.

"That girl knew what she wanted," Cotton says. "*And what she didn't want.* She made a hard decision—it had to be—because she knew what was best for her. People don't do that anymore, kid. They get suckered into shit and let it ruin their life."

Wow. This is not where I thought this was going. And yet he's right. He's so right about Laina.

"You gotta break some eggs to make some French toast," he says, laughing at his own joke. "I know that's not the saying, but I hate omelets."

"Not a big fan either." I laugh, too. "I get what you're saying."

More than you even know.

"Good. Now, let's get you back to work," Cotton says, spitting as he heads for his truck. "And if you tell anyone I said any of this shit, I'll call you a liar."

I look at Moe and chuckle.

You're not a liar at all, Cotton. Not even a little bit.

Chapter Ten

Laina

L aina

I dance across the kitchen as the oven buzzes. The house is filled with the scent of garlic and pasta sauce—with a kiss of burnt cake because I am not a baker. But even a cake shaved into an inch of its life to rid it of the crispy pieces can't break my spirits.

Not today. Not when I've had one of my life's most relaxing, amazingly boring, wonderfully mind-numbing days.

I slip on a mitt and remove the garlic bread from the oven.

The early evening sun warms the room without the stove's heat. Tall blades of grass sway in the breeze on the other side of the fence that separates Luke's yard from the pasture. Tall flowers provide pops of color along the fencerow, making the view resemble a painting.

In all my travels worldwide, including my own homes that I chose and designed, I've never been to a place quite like this. There's nothing fancy here. Some of it isn't even modern. The cabinets are from the eighties at best, and every tap in the house leaks. But instead of taking away from the property, it all somehow adds to it. It works together to create a place where nothing really matters except *being*. Breathing. *Living.*

And dammit if it's not glorious.

I check on the sauce I poured from a jar, hoping the spices I added to it actually enhance the flavor and don't take away from it. I glance at the cake—or *ruin it.*

"*Hey.*"

I shriek and jump back, hitting the stove with my hip. Luke grabs me before my arm lands in the simmering sauce, and we have a real mess to clean up.

"Dammit," I say, smacking Luke on the chest. "You just scared the shit out of me."

"I can tell." He grins. "What were you thinking about? Didn't you hear me pull up or come in?"

I drag my hand down his chest, relishing the contact as long as possible. "I was focusing."

"On what?"

"On making *you* dinner."

"I didn't know you knew how to cook."

"You haven't seen me in a long time. I can do lots of things that you don't know about."

Our gazes collide as soon as the words come out of my mouth. The corner of Luke's mouth tugs toward the ceiling.

"I may have you prove that," he says before walking away.

I heave a breath. "Don't look at the cake. It's not a good example of my talents."

He examines my handiwork with a smirk. "I'd fucking hope not. What happened to this thing?"

"Has anyone ever told you it's not smart to get lippy with the cook? I could poison you, and you'd never know it."

He rolls his eyes. "I'll take my chances."

"You like living on the wild side, huh?"

Luke just laughs.

I turn off the stove and give the pasta a final swish. "How was work? And why don't you smell like shit?"

"I came in and went straight to the shower."

"No, you did not. I would've heard you."

"Well, I heard your acapella rendition of 'Roadhouse Blues.'" He shrugs. "If I was going to make something up, that's not the song I would've led with as my first guess."

Shit. Maybe he was here, and I didn't hear him.

"What did you do today?" he asks, taking two glasses from the cupboard. "Anything fun? Do I have any privacy left?"

"Not a thing." I giggle. "I went through every drawer, closet, and corner of this place. I know everything about you."

"Good."

I take out two plates. "Good?"

"Yeah. Now you can reply in kind over dinner."

His smile warms my heart.

We move silently around the kitchen, handing each other plates and silverware without missing a beat. We then fill our plates, grab our drinks, and sit at the table by the door.

"There were three deer outside today," I say, pointing at the fencerow. "They stood there forever like they weren't scared at all."

"I don't let anyone hunt out here, so we see a lot of them."

I grin. "I love that you protect the wildlife. That's such a green flag."

He laughs. "A green flag, huh?"

"Yeah. If you have an online dating profile, you should put that in your bio." I drag my finger through the air. "I protect baby deer." I shrug. "It would get you lots of swipes."

He tears his garlic bread and stuffs half a piece in his mouth. I wait for him to comment on my observation, but he doesn't. Worse, I think he knows that I want him to admit whether he does or does not use dating websites and is intentionally screwing with me.

Bastard.

I sigh. "Fine. I'll ask. Do you use dating sites?"

His laughter is rich and warm. I could listen to it forever.

"What does it matter to you?" he asks.

"I'm just curious."

"Are you going to make a profile and stalk me there, too?"

I gasp. "I don't stalk you online. I just watch some of your videos."

He hums.

I hum right back.

"No, I don't use dating sites," he says, rolling his eyes. "I tried them once, and I saw enough weird shit the first weekend that I deleted it. People are fucked up."

"You should see some of the letters and gifts people send me. I had a guy send me ten used condoms once in the mail."

Luke's eyes widen. "That's gross."

"I know. Another guy sent me a tooth. I've had fingernail clippings, voodoo dolls, and someone sent me a live baby scorpion."

He sets the other half of his bread down. "You don't open that shit, do you?"

"No. It all goes to a post office box, and someone on my team opens it all. We're really careful about it."

He shakes his head like he can't believe it.

"I got my luggage and phone today," I say.

"How'd that go down?"

"Gavin met Stephanie on a random street in Brickfield. She basically threw it in his trunk and jetted away. Then Gavin brought it to me after stopping at the gas station, The Wet Whistle, and Chase's to make sure he wasn't being followed."

He nods like he's not surprised, which surprises me. But I don't say anything. I don't want him to think I'm overthinking things.

I scoop up a forkful of spaghetti. "I had the best day being here all alone. I can't think of the last time I was truly alone."

"Really?"

"I've been *alone* at home before, but that's semantics. Cameras monitor all the exits, and men patrol the grounds at all hours. Since people can look up my addresses online, they do. Those situations can get hairy."

The lines around Luke's eyes wrinkle.

"What about you?" I ask. "How was your day? What happened in the horseshoeing business?"

Luke takes a drink of tea. But before he can answer, his phone rings.

"Fuck. I should've turned this off before we sat down," he says, looking at the screen. "It's Mom. I'll call her back."

"No, answer it."

He looks up, surprised.

"Answer it," I say, nodding my insistence. "Always talk to your mom if she wants to talk to you."

A slow smile slips across his lips as he turns on the speakerphone. "Hi, Momma."

"Where have you been?" Maggie Marshall asks her son. "I waited for you all day to come and get some beans and cornbread."

He winks at me. "Mrs. Marshall, I don't like your tone."

"*Lucas Marshall*, I'll kick your behind if you call me that again."

Luke laughs. "Settle down. I'm only kidding."

I sit back and listen to them chatter back and forth.

The Marshalls have always shared a close bond. Maggie and Lonnie, Luke's parents, always ensured a strong connection between their children—and it stuck. I always loved going to their house. As soon as you walk in, you're surrounded by an indescribable *goodness*. They fill your stomach with food, your heart with laughter, and your soul with love. You can't walk away from the Marshalls and not leave feeling better than you did when you arrived.

Strangely enough, that was one of the things I missed about home when I moved to Nashville. Not my own childhood home or walking into my mother's kitchen. It was walking into the Marshall world where people connected. People cared. It's where people simply love on you because they know you well and love you unconditionally.

"Next week, I promise you I'll be at church," Luke says, rolling his eyes at me.

I smile at him.

"You better be," Maggie says. "You've missed three weeks in a row. One more week, and it'll constitute a habit. It's been a long while since I showed up at your house and honked my horn until you came out for church, but I'll do it again."

"What has gotten into you?" Luke asks, laughing. "Did you get into the communion wine again?"

I snort, holding a hand over my mouth so Maggie doesn't hear me.

"*Lucas.*" She sighs heavily. "I need to go. You're turning me gray."

"Why do I get blamed for everything? *It's always me.* Never Chase, the one who gets in tall buckets and plays with electricity all day. It's never Gavin, the bartender. You never blame Mallet, and he gets paid to punch people. And God knows it's not Kate."

"Be good. I love you, Luke."

"Love you, Momma."

"Say your prayers."

"I will. Good night."

"Good night, baby boy."

I wait until Luke ends the call to speak.

"Aw, Luke. That was the sweetest thing I've ever heard."

He takes a bite of his spaghetti. "What part? The one where she said I'm turning her gray or the part where she called me her baby boy?" He shakes his head. "She's confused, I think. She doesn't make sense."

"Oh, I think she makes perfect sense. You're the baby boy, so you're the one turning her gray."

"Technically, Gavin is the youngest boy in the family." His brows rise. "See? She makes zero sense."

I laugh. "I wish my mother was like Maggie. I can't even remember the last time my mom called me."

His chewing slows. "Really?"

"Really. Once Dad and I started ... not seeing eye to eye on every-

76

thing, she checked out of my life." I poke at a chunk of meat in the sauce on my plate. "We were never super close anyway, but we're even less close now. I don't know whether Dad made her choose sides or if she just isn't interested in me anymore. Whatever it is, before last weekend, I had only seen my mother a handful of times over the past year."

Luke reaches over the table and takes my hand. His thumb strokes my palm. The simple gesture springs tears in my eyes because I can't remember the last time someone saw me, saw my pain, and reached out—literally or physically.

"I don't know anything about being a mother or a parent," he says softly. *"But I know you."*

I stare into his eyes and hold on to them for dear life.

He whispers a laugh. "You're so fucking strong."

"Why is that funny?"

He squeezes my hand before releasing it.

"I had a long conversation with Cotton today," he says, shifting in his seat. "He just found out he has cancer."

"I'm sorry, Luke."

"Yeah. I'm sorry for him. He's so wily and energetic that it's hard to believe he's that sick." He blows out a breath. "Anyway, he told me about this girl who was supposed to get married in Brickfield and she brought half of California with her."

My stomach drops.

Luke smiles. "And he told me that he respected the bride."

What? "Seriously?"

"He said she knew what she wanted—and didn't want—and made a hard decision because it was best for her. He was pretty proud of her."

"Does he know me?" I ask, my cheeks flushing.

"Nope." He leans forward, resting his elbows on the edge of the table. "You are very impressive, Ms. Kelley. I'm sure you intimidate a lot of people. *And that isn't your problem.*"

"It feels like my problem sometimes."

He grins. "Well, it's not. And if you ever need a reminder, call me."

"You mean I can't just stalk your videos on Social?"

"Would you like me to start making videos talking directly to you?"

I laugh. "*Stephanie would die.*"

He sits back and crosses his arms over his chest. His smile is smug.

"What?" I ask, prodding him.

"I'm just imagining the hottest pop star in the world lying in her tour bus at night watching videos of me."

"Just think. Now you can imagine the hottest pop star in the world cooking you dinner in your kitchen."

His lips press together. "I've already done that."

"What?" I laugh. "You have?"

"I've thought about that woman cooking me dinner and dragging me to watch horrible plays in Indianapolis. And I've thought about her trying to get me to adopt a puppy from the fair."

My heart swells.

"And I've thought about teaching that woman to drive a stick shift, painting her fingernails when she broke her arm, and how she screamed at the top of her lungs at every jump-scare in scary movies."

I hold his gaze. "You have?"

"Of course I have."

My blood pressure rises as I lift from my seat. I'm not sure where I'm going or what I'm doing, but I know I can't sit any longer. I'm too fidgety, my skin too riddled with goose bumps to act natural.

"Do you know what else I thought about?" I ask.

"What's that?"

He watches me lean into the bend of the cabinets, resting my back against the ledge of the countertop. I should stop talking and leave this alone, but as I look into the eyes of the only man I've ever really loved, I can't.

"I thought about what life might've been like if I hadn't moved to Nashville," I say softly.

"I think about that every damn day."

He moves slowly but deliberately across the kitchen. A rush of heat cascades over my body, and I hold my breath until he stops inches before me.

Luke licks his lips. "This is why I said it would be a terrible idea for you to stay here."

"Is this really that awful?"

"It will be when you leave."

I take a shaky breath. "But I'm not leaving tonight."

He holds my face in his hands and stands against me. I look up at him with anticipation and expectation, practically begging him to break the barrier between us and kiss the hell out of me.

His thumbs slide along my jaw, and the calluses scrape against my skin. A bolt of energy fires directly to the apex of my thighs, and I stand on my tiptoes, ready and willing.

I want this. I need this. *I want and need him.*

The only thing that makes sense in my life is Luke Marshall. I don't understand how it came to this—how we got here—and it boggles my mind that this is even real.

But it's real. *He's real.* I've never been more certain about anything in my life. I don't care about the complications, although I know there will be some. I only care about being connected to him in a way I've never been connected with anyone else. I've buried so much of my pain, hidden it from the vultures swooping through my life, for many years.

I also hid the sense of feeling complete.

I've hidden it all because acknowledging it only brings on the hurt.

"I want nothing more than to carry you upstairs and show you exactly how much I've missed you," he says, searching my eyes.

"Please do."

His lips twitch. "I don't want to take advantage of you, Laina."

"You're not. I promise."

He gives me a soft, crooked smile.

"Luke, *please*," I say, my tone thick with desperation. "Give me tonight."

He pulls me into his chest, pressing his lips to my forehead. His heart pounds against my palms.

"It's been a long couple of days," he says, pulling back. "Why don't we take it easy tonight? Just hang out. And if you're still into it tomorrow, I'll assume you won't regret it. Because I can't be a regret. I just can't."

My core burns, refusing to accept his offer, but my heart is a sap. *How can I be mad at the man for wanting to do right by me? It's sweet —annoying and frustrating, but sweet all the same.*

"I hate you," I say, squeezing my thighs together in a futile attempt to quell the ache between my legs.

He laughs. "You've said that once to me already today."

"I feel it coming on a few more times before the day ends."

"Why don't you go get a shower and let me clean up dinner? Then we can watch a movie or something."

I roll my eyes and walk around him. "I might lie in your room and read a book."

"You get the couch, remember?"

"Absolutely not. You could've joined me in bed." I stop at the doorway and turn to him. "And I would've made it worth your while."

His nostrils flare.

"But you said no."

I flash him a sweet smile and head up the stairs.

I wonder if he can make it all night ...

Chapter Eleven

L aina

The fucker made it all night.

Chapter Twelve

Laina

"Come on," Luke says, thrusting a cup of coffee into my hands. "Cheer up. It's gonna be a beautiful day."

"Let's see how you feel about that when you're wearing my drink."

He laughs, enjoying my irritation entirely too much for his safety.

In Luke's defense, he did let me sleep in. In my defense, I could've been tired out a lot more easily if he would've given in and fucked me last night. Even though that might not have been in our best interests, particularly because I'll need to leave once the dust settles. But he was adamant, so maybe, *just maybe*, Luke Marshall isn't interested in me.

At some point since I've been away from Peachwood Falls, it seems Luke has become a choir boy.

Damn him.

I love a thoughtful man. *It's so sexy.* It's such a turn-on. But it's less appealing when you need an orgasm as badly as you need air, and the man you want to rail you grows a conscience.

"You could try to be a little nicer to me." He smirks. "I even got up bright and early and drove to Chase's to borrow a pair of Kennedy's boots just for you."

"I feel it coming on."

"What are you talking about?"

I lean forward and whisper, "*I hate you.*"

All he does is laugh.

I down the rest of the caffeine and then follow him outside. He's right—it is a beautiful day. The sun is high and bright, the birds are singing in the trees, and a perfect breeze rolls gently across the driveway as we approach the barn.

"You're in luck," he says.

"That's exactly what I feel. *Lucky.*"

He rolls his eyes. "The weather has been really nice, so the horses have been in the pasture most of the time. The stalls aren't awful."

"Yay."

"Come on," he says, bumping me with his elbow. "This is going to be so much fun."

"Luke, let me share something with you. Some things are fun, and others are not. Things that take place involving horse shit are not in the fun column. Ever. Okay? Let it go."

"You're testy this morning."

I glare at him as he opens the doors to the barn.

"Being mean isn't going to make this go any faster," he says.

"Trust me. I know. For the past twelve hours, I've thought very mean things about you, and they've dragged on."

His eyes sparkle as he walks me back until my backside touches the wall. I refuse to let him think he's breaking me.

His hands are planted on either side of my head, caging me in. He's so close that I can smell the toothpaste and coffee on his breath. I lift my chin in defiance.

"Why are you so mad, Pumpkin?" he asks, teasing me.

"Don't call me that when you're being mean."

"*I'm not being mean.*" He grins. "I told you I just wanted to give you a little space. It's the right thing to do."

"No, Luke, the right thing to do would've been to fuck me so hard that I stop thinking about all the crap that happened this week. But thank you so very much."

The grin twists into a darker smile. It sends a shiver down my spine.

That's it. This is where I want you.

"That's not why I'm mad at you, though," I say, pretending to fix his shirt so I can touch him. "I'm quite capable of taking care of myself. I do it all the time." I act like I dust something off his shoulder. "I'm just a little unhappy about having to get up so early, and I really hate horse shit. So why don't we—"

"No." He pushes away from me and heads toward a storage room. "You're cleaning these stalls with me."

"*Luke,*" I whine. "Come on. Let me cheer you on instead."

He hands me a really big rake-like thing. "Have you done this before?"

"Are you listening to me?"

"No."

"Red flag."

He tries not to laugh.

"I'll sing for you," I say.

"No, Laina."

He plops several other tools into a wheelbarrow and starts toward the stalls.

"Dude, people pay me to sing, and I'm willing to do it for you for free. *A full concert.* I won't stop as long as you're working." I follow him. "You're getting a hell of a deal."

He opens the gate. "See the piles of poop?"

"This is so freaking gross."

He grins. "See them?"

"Yeah. I see 'em."

"First, use your manure fork to lift the poop and give it a little shake to get the clean bedding off. Then you'll put it in the wheelbarrow," he says.

"I can't believe I'm doing this," I mutter.

"Then sweep all the bedding away from the pee spots. Then take the shovel and put the pee-soaked bedding in the wheelbarrow."

"I'm noticing a trend."

He ignores me. "Give the pee areas a quick spray of odor eliminator and then brush all the bedding still in here over those areas. Then we'll put new bedding down." He smiles at me. "Got it?"

"I really thought you were joking about this."

I stare him down as I step into the stall. "You know, this is making me rethink leaving Tom."

Luke turns away. "You'd be dealing with a pile of shit either way."

"Okay, I'll give you that one. That was funny."

He turns on music and starts to work on the stall beside me.

It takes a while, but I get into the groove. It's not as bad as I feared and not nearly as stinky. By the time I get to the urine, *I'm not enjoying myself*, but it is a little satisfying. Strangely, we haven't spoken for over half an hour, which reminds me of all the times we just hung out years ago simply to be with each other. We knew each other so well then. *How much of that has changed?*

What do I really know about this man today?

"Do you enjoy being a farrier?" I ask.

"Yeah. Of course. It's all I ever wanted to do."

"I wondered. Sometimes people change their minds, but they're stuck doing what they're doing that pays the bills."

"What about you? Do you like performing?"

I scoop up the last clump of urine, then mist the areas with deodorizing spray.

"Laina?"

"Yeah, I do," I say, trying to find the words to describe my messy thoughts. "I actually love putting on shows and the theatrics of it. I love engaging with my fans, and hearing their stories, and listening to how my songs have impacted their lives. And I love songwriting and collaborating with other artists."

"But ..."

I sigh and set the spray next to the wheelbarrow. "But I'm tired."

The scraping from his stall halts.

"I love what I do, Luke. I'm so lucky, so blessed, and so grateful for the opportunity to do what I do. What an honor. But I don't want my job—and it very much is a job—to be my whole person *and all that I am.*"

He comes to the stall doorway beside mine and leans on his broom. His eyes are tender, full of concern, and it melts my heart right down to my—Kennedy's—boots.

"I'm a paycheck to everyone now," I say, my eyes filling with tears.

I've never said this aloud to anyone. I'm not sure I've even given myself the freedom to think this thought through. But as I hear the words, I know they're true. I can feel them release from my heart.

"My parents see me as a paycheck," I say. "Agents, publicists, managers. Backup designers. Set designers. Costume designers. Lighting crews. Security details. Property managers. Chefs. Those people's families. Accountants. Attorneys. I could go on and on."

"Then stop."

"I don't want to stop making music."

He leans the broom against the wall. "You don't have to stop making music. But you can also find a way to have a life outside of it. Laina, you don't exist to keep thousands of people's lives turning. And whoever made you feel like that can fuck off."

"If only I had a reason to have a farrier on tour with me. You could come and tell people that."

He laughs. "Find a way to get horses into your show, and I'm there."

"Don't tempt me."

We exchange a smile.

"I'll tell you what," I say, stretching my back. *Damn, this is hard work.* "You dump that load of crap wherever you put it. Then come back and I'll clean out the next one without complaining if you tell me stories."

"About what?"

I shrug. *Normal life.* "I don't know. Tell me what you do all day. Tell me why you shove all of your receipts into one drawer in the kitchen. Or explain why you have twenty-one cans of tomato soup."

"You really did go through everything."

"I told you I did."

He narrows his eyes, trying to decide whether I'm joking. I didn't go through *everything* in his house. But I'm not telling him that. I like to watch him squirm. It's fun. *He's fun.*

How could something that came so naturally between us for years still be there? How can this man make me feel more beautiful in pink boots and horse shit than a team of experts can make me feel in glam and couture?

It's the mystery of Luke Marshall.

"Walk with me," he says.

Luke pushes the soiled bedding out the far side of the barn. The sun hits us immediately, warming my face. *Man, I've missed the sun, too.*

The realization that I haven't relaxed in the sun more than a few times over the past few years wallops me. I'm normally in a studio or rehearsals. Sometimes I'm in bed due to a late meeting and then wake up and scramble to start the day. Even if I have a day off and am in a location to enjoy the sunshine without skyscrapers, Tom's voice is in my head about avoiding the sun so I don't screw up my complexion with freckles and sun damage.

How did I put up with his shit for so long? And how does no one else in the world see him like that?

We move quietly down a path until we come upon a manure compost pile. He deposits the fresh load onto the mound.

"It's been a long time now," he says as we return to the barn. "I can't truthfully remember why at this point, but everyone was saying the world was going to end."

We slow as a butterfly flutters along in front of us.

"I thought it was bullshit. And I was right," he says, chuckling. "But Gavin believed it. He had a solid six months where he was certain the world was ending due to some old calendar someone found somewhere. I don't know. It was ridiculous."

"I never imagined Gavin as a conspiracy-theory type."

He snorts. "If Gavin loves two things, one is beef jerky, and the other is a good conspiracy theory."

"Good to know."

"We all blew him off. Mallet even left the family text thread at one point because Gavin would start the day with a *countdown to the end*—and he was dead serious."

"Oh, wow," I say, laughing.

"Chase had to threaten him to shut up around Kennedy because he was starting to freak her out. As this very random date on the calendar approached, Gavin started showing up at our houses with ... stuff."

"What kind of stuff?"

"I think Chase got cases of Pop-Tarts and something really off the wall. Pineapple juice, maybe? I can't remember."

I laugh, gazing up in appreciation of Luke's rugged profile.

"Kate lived close then, and I think she got something like tortilla chips and baked beans," Luke says. "Mom and Dad got those little wieners in a can." He looks at me and grins. "*A lot of them.*"

"I can see ways of whittling down the Pop-Tarts. Pineapple juice is good in mixed drinks. Tortilla chips and baked beans can be used. I mean, it might take a while, but you could use those in everyday life. It's the wieners for me."

"There's a joke there, and I'm letting it go. I want you to know that."

I shove him, making him laugh. "Is this story going anywhere? Or did you want me to walk into a wiener joke?"

"I was trying to get to the tomato soup."

"Well, get there, then."

He pushes the wheelbarrow back into the barn.

"That's what I got from Gav—tomato soup. Twenty-however-many cans of it," Luke says. "Definitely better than the wieners, but I would've loved those Pop-Tarts. I tried to barter with Chase, but he wasn't having it. He said it was the only useful thing Gavin had ever done for him, and he and Kennedy were eating them. I'm stuck with the cans of soup that have probably expired."

I laugh. Actually, it's more like a cackle. The thought of all those wieners totally amuses me. And Luke still has the cans of soup.

But while I find amusement in the story, I'm also ... *sad*. In leaving Luke, this is what I missed. I might have been here to use those cans of soup. I might have been the recipient of something equally bizarre. *How fun would that have been.*

"I wish I had siblings."

"Uh, no, you don't."

"I do," I say emphatically. "You have such a bond with your brothers and Kate. Heck, you and Gavin even seem to have a bond with Kennedy. I have a bond with no one. It's just me out here."

We stop by the next two stalls. Luke dusts his hands off and looks at me.

"What?" I ask.

"How would you feel about seeing my parents?"

This is not a question I was expecting.

"No pressure," Luke says. "I know you're skittish about seeing people right now, and I get it. I respect it. But they won't tell anyone, and I know they'd love to see you. Mom is gonna be pissed that she didn't know you were here. She'll think we stole a reason from her to make a casserole."

I laugh, the sentiment like a rush of sunshine on my soul.

To see Maggie and Lonnie again would be like curling up in my favorite blanket. I wish I would've kept in contact with them over the years. They were a piece of good in my life, and I'm certain they would've offered me advice when I needed it the most throughout the years. But it felt too odd, *too sad*, to stay in touch with them after Luke and I fell apart.

Lonnie wouldn't have tolerated Tom Waverly, and he sure as hell wouldn't have allowed me to get engaged to him without a long chat —with both of us. Even if I wasn't dating Luke anymore, I know he would've said something. Maggie, too. It's too bad that didn't happen.

And it's also too bad that I've missed so much since I left. Even if I gained a career and a whole life by leaving, I lost, too. Because in my heart, Peachwood Falls—the Marshalls—feels like home.

"You know what, Luke? I want to see them. It would be nice to say hello again."

"Okay. But I'm not responsible if Mom gets too squirrely on you. You heard her last night. She's getting uncontrollable in her old age."

"Don't you let her hear you say that."

He hands me a shovel and picks up another one.

"I tell her shit like that sometimes just to wind her up. It's a good cardio workout." He winks at me. "Now, let's get these last four cleaned, refill them with clean bedding, and get out of here."

"Sounds like a plan to me."

We trade a final smile and get busy.

Chapter Thirteen

Laina

I step out of the shower and wrap myself in the fluffiest towel in the cabinet. Then I quickly dry my hair with another one.

Luke told me stories most of the day, just like I requested. The time flew by, and I surprisingly didn't hate barn work as much as I thought I would. We stopped for a sandwich midafternoon, and then he did paperwork in the barn office while I swept the floors and cleaned the water buckets and feeders.

The silence gave me time to move my body—without a trainer screaming at me—and to unload my mental burdens.

I take in my reflection in the mirror. The rosiness in my cheeks looks nice. Even without concealer, I don't look like a zombie—a huge surprise. Most importantly, when I look into my eyes, I don't see a woman worried about how the pieces of her life will fall in line. I see someone who might trust the process and herself to make it work no matter what.

When I open the door, steam billows into the hallway. I step onto the carpet and notice Luke standing at the bottom of the stairs. His hair is wet from the shower he took while I swept off the back porch. I decided to do it since I was filthy anyway.

A pair of sweatpants hangs low on his hips. He's shirtless—*because, of course, he is.* His feet are bare, too.

It's been too long since I've had sex. I'm not strong enough for this level of visual temptation.

His chest is wide and dusted with hair, and his shoulders rise to his neck in thick layers of muscle. Lines are etched into his abdomen imperfectly because they were created by hard work, not a gym. His arms are a map of hills and valleys as one muscle runs into the next, and the tattoos on his left shoulder that I've only seen in a couple of shirtless videos online *are so fucking sexy* in person.

My lord.

The man is a work of art.

"I thought I heard the shower turn off," he says, one foot resting casually on the bottom step. Mischief dances along his features. "I thought we could order a pizza for dinner. Figured you'd be too tired to help me make anything."

My skin tingles at the look in his eyes—the one that says he's been thinking about eating, and it has nothing to do with dinner.

I grin, easing my grip on the towel slightly so it drops low enough to expose the tops of my breasts. I pretend not to notice.

He notices, though. His gaze drops immediately to my chest.

"Good call," I say, squeezing my chest together. "I'm exhausted after everything today. I might even take a quick nap."

His gaze sears a path from my décolletage, up my neck, across my jaw, and to my eyes.

"Let me know if you need anything," I say coyly.

He licks his lips as I turn away and head for the bedroom.

By the time I reach the doorway, I'm practically panting. My heart pounds with anticipation. He wanted me last night—we both know it. I made it clear that I wanted him. The ball is in his court. *Will he pick it up?* I groan. *Please let him pick it up.*

I close the door and toss my towel on the bed. I reach for a cute leisurewear set in my suitcase when my attention falls on something else.

"Aha," I say, pulling it from the depths of my bag. A grin splits my cheeks. "This will do far more for me now than it would've on my honeymoon."

I slip on the emerald-green see-through baby doll-style lingerie and the tiniest thong known to man. The sides are cut, exposing my hips when I move. It was marketed as "fun and flirty," which is exactly what I need right now.

"Let's see what you think about this, Luke." I twirl in the mirror, watching how the fabric shifts to obscure my nipples one moment and then make them completely visible the next. "I hope this drives you crazy."

I move into the en suite and add some product to my hair and a touch of lip gloss to my pout. Then I add a coat of mascara, too. *Why not? Go big or go home.* I start to leave but turn back and give myself two squirts of perfume.

"Hey, Laina," Luke calls from the living room. "What do you want on the pizza?"

I find the matching robe with the satin edges and minutely thicker material. Then I slip it on.

"Here goes nothing," I whisper and open the door. "What did you say?"

"What do you want on your pizza?"

I peer down into the living room but can't see Luke. The television is on a sports channel, and his voice comes from not too far away. *He must be on the couch.*

Excitement blooms in my stomach as I reach the top of the stairs.

What will he say? What will his reaction be? I'm not the little girl he remembers.

"Pepperoni is good," I say, my voice perfectly detached. I don't look at him as I take the first step. "Anything but sardines and onions I can—"

"*Holy fuck.*"

I win. I lift my chin and pretend not to hear him clamor to sit upright. "Handle."

"For fuck's sake, Laina. *Damn.*"

I glance at him over my shoulder, knowing full well he's about to get a glimpse of my bare ass as I walk by. "What's wrong, Luke?"

"Stop it. *Just stop it,*" he says, the words ending on a growl. "No. Don't stop it. Come here instead."

"I'm going to get a glass of tea. Do you want anything?"

"Yeah. But it isn't tea."

He scrambles to his feet as I round the corner and out of his view.

I make myself a drink I'm wholly uninterested in to keep busy. I want him to want me. *I want him to sweat.*

"Did you order the pizza?" I ask sweetly. "I'm starving."

"I can't ... what?"

I look over my shoulder. He's leaning against the doorframe, his mouth agape.

"Pizza," I say slowly. "You were ordering pizza. Remember?"

"Nope. I don't." His gaze drags down my body inch by inch. "I don't even remember my name right now. *Damn, Laina. You are fucking gorgeous.*"

I grin. "Thanks. This is just a little something I found in my suitcase."

Luke runs a hand over his chin and laughs faintly. "I can't even find words. I feel like a fool."

"You are a fool. You could've had this last night, but you turned me down." I smile smugly and wink at him. "Now order the pizza so I can go to bed with a hot piece tonight."

"Is that how you're going to play this?"

"I'm not playing anything, Luke."

Even if he couldn't see my face, he would know unequivocally that I am, in fact, playing with him. I couldn't keep the taunt out of my voice if I tried. *And I try.*

"This isn't playing fair," he says.

"Life isn't fair."

"I was doing the right thing. I wanted to make sure you weren't doing something you'd regret."

I level my gaze at him. "Do you want to know what I think it was?"

"I just told you what it was."

"Hmm ... I don't think so." I lick my bottom lip. "I think you were making sure you weren't doing something *you'd* regret."

His eyes blaze.

"Called you out with that one, huh?" I ask. "I don't want to take anything away from you, so I'll admit that you were being a gentleman and giving me space to process the past few days. And from the bottom of my heart, I appreciate that. Thank you."

He shifts his weight.

"But I also think you have the same thoughts going through your head that I do," I say. "And you're afraid if we connect like this, if we have sex, that it'll hurt just as much as it did back then when we part."

"What's your solution to that?"

I smile at him. "I don't have one. But I've made some big, risky decisions lately. They haven't killed me yet. I might as well make one more. At least this time it won't hurt when you don't come for me. I'll already expect it."

"What are you talking about?" His face grows sober in a flash. "What do you mean when I don't come for you?"

"I really thought you'd come and see me. You said you would. But it doesn't matter now. We survived, and now we're here. We've had a lot of life experiences since then. I think we can decide whether to hook up or not."

"I have one problem with that."

"Now?"

He grins. "Yes, now."

"What? Hurry up. You still have to order the pizza."

"I think the pizza got put on the back burner." He blows out a breath. "Look, if we take things any further, it won't be a hookup for me."

My stomach drops to the floor.

"You have to know that going into it," he says, watching me closely. "I'm not saying ... I don't know what I'm saying, Laina. I understand how different our lives are and how each is important to us. But I can't just be exiled from your life again. I want you—I've always wanted you. Not a day has passed that I haven't wanted any part of you that you'd give me."

I struggle to catch a steady breath. My heart races as I wrap my head around what he's saying. *He's ... always wanted me? But he didn't find me. He let me go when I left. Luke didn't pursue me, so why is he saying this?*

"I've never exiled you from my life, Luke. I don't know why you're saying that."

His eyes narrow as he closes the gap between us.

"This is your call. You can stay here either way. Regardless of what happens in the next few minutes, I'll always be there for you." He swallows, his Adam's apple bobbing in his throat. "But if you really want to take this beyond a friendship, if only for this one night, it will change things for me. I'm not going to pretend it won't."

His confession makes my head spin. There is so much to unpack. *Why does he think I exiled him? And is he telling me he believes we should try again?*

Do I want that?

A million thoughts race through my mind at record speed. People will vilify me—they'll downright crucify me if anyone finds out that I slept with Luke this close to my runaway bride act. They'll think I've been cheating on Tom with Luke. The headlines will smear me and say that I led Tom on, and this is payback for what happened in Paris. That's how their small minds work. Because the press doesn't know about Luke. Somehow.

But my father knows about Luke.

He knows about Luke and *will actually* lose his brain if he hears that we've rekindled a relationship. I'm unsure if it will impact my brand deals or sponsorships. *Will my public relations team give up on me if I do this?*

Those thoughts weigh heavily on my mind as I stand before Luke. But as I look up into his handsome face, those beautiful, kind eyes, and into a soul I feel as connected to now as I ever have ... I don't care.

I just don't care.

Let them talk. They're going to anyway.

I've made so many decisions to make everyone else happy. This— Luke—will make me happy.

"Here's the thing," I say, running my hands across his chest. "I don't think what we have is just a friendship. I don't think it's ever been just that."

His breaths are shaky.

"And I've had many life experiences since I left this town, but none of them feel the way I feel when I'm with you," I say, smiling up at him. "I don't know what this looks like or how it would work. *If it can work.* But I am one thousand percent sure I won't wake up in the morning and regret this. I'll only regret it if we don't."

A slow smile slips across his face. "Well, Ms. Kelley, I'd hate to disappoint you."

Something tells me that won't happen.

Chapter Fourteen

L uke

"And I've had many life experiences since I left this town, but none of them feel the way I feel when I'm with you."

It's no wonder this woman has always owned my heart.

I study her, taking in her beauty and intelligence. Her honesty.

I've tried to resist her, but I can't. I want to make her feel good. I want to show her how special she is, how she's more than a paycheck and an avenue to exploit for personal gain. *Although I'll definitely gain from this interaction.*

My heart pounds.

But I stand to lose a lot, too.

Memories of the hurt after she left before are just below the surface, reminding me that I might find myself in that situation again. It would be worse this time. I'm not sure I would survive it in one piece. But as I take her in and consider turning her away, that's impossible.

I've loved her for too long.

Loving her is as natural as breathing. I don't have to try. And, if I try not to love her, I fail and end up miserable, clinging to the pieces of my life that still make sense and hoping that something changes someday.

Maybe that day is today.

I take a long, deep breath.

I can only hope that Laina feels this way, too. I can only hope that she'll want to try for more. I can only hope that she'll want the happiness that has eluded me since she left—happiness that I think she hasn't been able to find elsewhere, either—and will decide that it's worth the risk we'll have to take to try to recapture it. Because one thing is clear to me. My happiness only exists with Laina Kelley.

She landed here for a reason. And maybe that reason is so I can make her mine.

Chapter Fifteen

Laina

"Sit down," Luke says. The words are a command and not a request.

A chill slips down my spine as anticipation starts to get the best of me.

We've done this before—too many times to count. I've been under him, on top of him, and beside him. *But it's never been like this.*

This Luke, the one staring at me with darkened eyes and a delicious smirk, isn't the sweet and playful guy who took my virginity. This man is confident. Deliberate. And, if I'm really lucky, he'll take playful to a whole new level.

"May I start by sitting on your face?" I ask, grinning innocently at him.

"Later. Sit in a chair."

I'm confused about how this will work if I'm sitting at the kitchen table, but I'm curious enough to play along.

"I'm big into foreplay," I say, facing away from him. "But I'm not really understanding what you're—oh, wow. *Wait.* What are you doing?"

Before I can begin the question, my hands are held together behind the chair. My jaw goes slack, and my core heats to a boil.

"Do you trust me?" he asks, his lips brushing the shell of my ear.

I shiver. "Depends."

"What if I promise you that I'll make you come?"

"Absolutely. And whatever word means more than that if you make me come faster. I—oh!"

Before I can finish the thought, a black rope cinches around my middle just above my belly button and sucks me against the chair.

"Luke," I say, my heart racing. "What are you doing?"

"Just playing with you a little bit. If you want me to let you go, I will. Just say the word."

I try to wiggle my hands but can't move them at all. It heightens my other senses, delivering a delicious new level of anticipation.

"I can't play with you if I can't move," I say, lifting a brow. "Complicated thing to understand, I know."

He moves the chair so I'm facing the refrigerator. Then he pulls a chair in front of me and sits.

"I didn't say *you* were playing with *me*," he says, enjoying himself. "For a woman who writes song lyrics, you sure don't understand basic English."

"Very funny."

He grins. "My God, you are beautiful."

I wiggle against the rope again.

"Stop it," he says, laughing. "You can't slip out of that."

"You don't know that."

"This is the kind of stuff I do for a living. So I do know that."

Oh. Good point. "What are we doing here?"

"Remember a little while ago when you got out of the shower and taunted me?"

I gulp.

"And remember last night when we were watching the movie and you kept *accidentally* rubbing your foot on my cock?" he asks.

Unfortunately, yes.

"Oh, I have one," he says. "What about when you came downstairs in lingerie and acted like you just wanted a piece of fucking pizza?"

Oops.

"This is my version of that," he says, grinning. "This is called ... paybacks are a bitch."

"Don't be vengeful. You don't want to be that guy. Just let me go, and I'll ride your cock. You won't be sorry. I promise."

"Nah. I'm good."

He scoots his chair so close that his knees frame mine. The soft fabric of his sweatpants brushes across my bare skin. I try again to free my hands to no avail.

His palms cup the sides of my face. They're rough against my cheeks, providing yet another sensation.

My legs squeeze together as my arousal coats the inside of my thighs. *I need him. I need him so damn bad.*

He lowers his mouth to mine. I moan as he nips at my bottom lip. The twinge of pain cuts through the riot inside me, rocketing me back to the present. I open my eyes to find his waiting for the contact before he crushes his mouth against mine.

The world stops spinning.

Luke takes control, working his lips against mine. My jaw falls lax as I struggle to remember to breathe. He takes that opportunity to explore my mouth with his tongue.

Fire spreads from my core, raising my temperature to dangerous levels. When he finally pulls back, I'm lightheaded. *Breathe, Laina.*

"Please let me go," I say, panting.

"Not a chance."

He pushes my robe off my shoulders and down my arms as far as it'll go. My nipples strain against the thin fabric of my lingerie, desperate for attention.

They don't have to wait long.

He takes his time removing each breast from the fabric, letting them hang over the cup.

"You're perfect," he says, sweeping his gaze over me. "You are absolutely perfect."

He places a hand between my legs, urging them apart, and I sink against him, whimpering—begging for him to touch me.

"I would be perfect if you'd make me come," I say.

"You're going to. Don't worry about that."

"Prove it."

He laughs, sliding a finger inside me. It takes me by surprise, and I yelp, both from the jolt and from the pleasure. I grind my pussy against him as hard as I can.

"You have no idea how hot it is to watch you fight not to fall apart on my hand," he says.

I lean my head back, causing the ends of my hair to swish against my hands.

I never imagined that I would enjoy being tied to a chair and fingered, but it's so fucking good. Not being able to move adds a layer of trust and another layer of suspense. *What will he do next? Where will he touch me? When will I—*"Fuck!"

The pad of his thumb rubs small circles around my clit. Each swipe across the swollen bud sends a bolt of electricity running through my veins.

"Do you want to come on my fingers?" he asks.

"Keep doing that, and I will." I squeeze my eyes shut, rolling my hips as he finger fucks me. "This feels so good, Luke. So damn good."

He sucks my right nipple into his mouth and pulls his finger out of me.

I start to object, but the pleasure radiating from my chest steals the words. Nips. Flicks. The pad of his tongue massages my tightened bud—but I wish I could reach for him. Touch his skin, feel how soft yet hard he is. I've always loved the feel of his body against mine. *This is torture.*

He pulls away, sitting back and watching me as he pops his fingers into his mouth.

"How do I taste?" I ask.

He leans forward and slides his tongue through my mouth. I bite it, sucking his tongue before he can pull it away. When he settles back in his seat, his eyes are blazing.

"What do you think?" he asks. "How *do* you taste?"

"I don't have a lot to compare it to. Why don't you take your cock out and put it in my mouth?"

His grin is salacious. "Is that what you want? Do you want me to fuck your mouth?"

"You can start there. But it won't be the only thing you fuck tonight."

Whoa. Who has taken control of my tongue tonight? I never spoke to Tom during sex like this. Maybe at the beginning when things were fun-*ish*. But tonight, the words are pouring out of me without thought. It's natural. *And I don't want to hold back.*

He stands, the veins in his temples pulsing, and pulls out his cock. It's heavy in his hand—thick and veiny. The head is purple as he squeezes the base. A bead of pre-cum glistens on the tip.

I hold his gaze. "Give it to me. Let me taste you."

His hands wind through my hair as he slides his length toward my mouth. I meet him midway, flicking my tongue across the head. The fluid is warm and salty—and the groan that erupts from his throat makes me feel powerful.

I suck the head as he presses himself past my lips.

He hisses as he hits the back of my throat.

I lick the head, spitting down the shaft before he plunges into my mouth again.

"*You feel so good,*" he says, the words raw. "I want to come down your throat so fucking bad."

I hum around his cock, sheathing my teeth and taking him down my throat again.

His fingers dig into my scalp, and his hips rock against me harder.

My spit drips down his balls and falls onto my legs. I keep sucking the head, winding my tongue around it, and making as much contact with my mouth to stimulate him in every way. My eyes start to burn as his pace picks up.

It was never like this with him before. It's never been like this with anyone, not that there have been that many. I've been treated like some glass doll that might break. Only Luke knows that's not true —that I wanted him to play with me.

I want to feel *everything*.

I start to gag as he pushes too far, and he stops and removes his cock from my mouth. He kisses me deep and hard before pulling away.

His eyes are wild, his breathing as erratic as mine. Our gazes connect, and we smile.

And *that feeling*—the warmth and intimacy of his smile—is the best so far.

He unfastens the rope, and my shoulders fall forward. My wrists burn from the bite of the material holding them together, but I don't have time to worry about that because Luke is picking me up and setting me on the table.

"I have to get a condom," he says.

"Don't."

He stops mid-turn and lifts a brow.

I trust you. You are the only man, maybe the only person, I've ever truly trusted. I smile at him. *And nothing has changed.*

"I'm on birth control," I say. "And I'm good to go."

"Are you sure? I'm good. That's not a problem."

I grab his sides and bring him closer to me. I gaze up at him. "I want to feel you—all of you. I want to feel you come deep inside me."

"Fucking hell."

He urges me back until I'm lying on the table. I grab the half-wall ledge to brace myself.

"I want this too badly, and I've wanted it for too long, that I won't last long," he says.

105

"Same. I need to come. Now."

He grins, sliding my thong down my legs. "We'll get this first round out of our systems so we can relax, and then we can do it again and take our time?"

"I hope you mean we can do it many more times and take our time," I say, wrapping my legs around his waist. "Now stop talking."

"You're very bossy."

"I know what I want."

I'm not sure what I said that earns his smile, but I'll take it. *And I also take his cock.*

My legs are over his shoulders, and my ass hangs at the edge of the table when Luke thrusts inside me.

"*That,*" I say, my legs trembling. "Give me that."

"You like this?" He leans back, then plows into me again. "Like that?"

"*Like that.*"

He repeats the motion. Again. And again.

My arms go weak as I try to keep my head from ramming into the wall. My back burns as it squeaks against the table. The back of my pussy throbs as it takes impact after impact, and it's the most glorious, delicious feeling ever.

"*Harder,*" I say, clenching my teeth. "*Fuck me, Luke.*"

"You want fucked? You got it."

I scream as he grips my waist, my legs flailing over his shoulders, and drives himself into me without mercy. I hold my breasts as they bounce with each thrust and close my eyes as the pressure becomes almost too much.

"How hard do you want it?" he asks, his fingers digging into my skin. "*Tell me how hard you want it.*"

"Just like that." The words are hard to get out. "Just ... like that."

"I'm going to come," he says.

"Don't stop! Please! One more—*fuck!*"

My body shakes as tiny constellations float through my vision. My legs tremble so hard that I can't stop them. Beads of sweat drip from Luke's forehead onto my stomach as he holds himself inside me and fills me with his cum.

I try to laugh, but it sounds more like a whine as I fall unceremoniously back to earth.

Luke's arms give out, and his shoulders sag.

I carefully pull my legs off him.

He pants, an ear-to-ear smile on his face. "I don't think I've ever come that hard in my life."

"I assure you that I haven't." I struggle to sit up. "I still can't see clearly."

Luke scoops me up, cradling me like a baby, and presses a kiss against my forehead.

"I need the next round to be somewhere soft," I say, yawning.

"Did you get hurt?"

I trail my fingertips down his cheek. "Not yet."

He kisses me again and carries me upstairs.

Chapter Sixteen

Laina

"Look," I say, my voice sleepy. "The sun is coming up."

Luke brushes his fingertips over my arm as I snuggle into him. "You kept me busy tonight." He pauses. "Last night? What's the right word?"

I laugh and stretch, my muscles screaming for rest. Being with Luke makes Pilates seem like a walk in the park. Only, walks in the park aren't this fun.

"Who knows," I say, curling up against him again. "Just say that I kept you busy. Point made."

"You kept me *very busy*." He chuckles into the top of my head. "I didn't know I had that much stamina. You must admit, I was impressive."

"That you were. *All five times*. You were so impressive, in fact, that whenever you're ready to go again, just let me know."

His chest shakes as he chuckles again. "I need a nap and a snack first. Unless you want to put my cock in your mouth. I'm sure you can convince it to go another round."

His hand snakes around my side and grabs my boob.

"I was kidding," I say, grinning. "I need a nap, a snack, and a cold compress, I think."

Muted rays of sunlight flicker into the room. The trees are illuminated from behind, creating a painting-worthy picture in the distance. The world slowly awakens, greeting us with the coziest, warmest *good morning*.

I yawn, wiggling around until I'm comfortable. I can't help but notice the ink on the top part of his arm. Each thin line is crisp, marrying different shapes into one beautiful, intricate design. Tattoos aren't something I would've thought Luke would do. Yet, somehow, it's perfect.

"Tell me about these," I say, tracing lines in his skin.

"What do you want to know?"

"I don't know. What made you get them? What do they mean? Or are they random stuff you plucked off an artist's wall?"

He takes a deep breath. "They all mean something."

The faint catch in his voice makes me pause. There's a chance he doesn't want to share this with me. After all, I haven't been in his life for a long time. Maybe some of these are to mark special events in his life that don't involve me.

As true as it is, my heart still squeezes tight. I'm not mad—that would be ridiculous. I'm not hurt because I was engaged to another man, for heaven's sake. But my heart hurts for the years we didn't share—for all the time we spent apart, for the pain we caused—and for the wounds we didn't help each other heal.

For the life we lived without one another.

"I think most guys get tattoos of really cool shit," he says, running his fingers through my hair. "Mine are pretty dorky."

I smile against him. "I definitely want to know now."

He holds his arm so we both can see it better.

"You better not make fun of me," he says.

"No promises."

He rolls his eyes. "The outside line is a horseshoe. That should be self-explanatory. And there's a *p* wrapped around the top of it for Poppy."

I find the letter and press my fingertip against it.

"Inside the horseshoe are things that remind me of all the important people in my life," he says, clearing his throat. "There's a daisy for my mom. She's always growing something in her garden. Flowers or those damn roses that make me bleed when she cons me into coming over and pruning them for her."

I chuckle softly.

"There's a flag for my dad to honor his time in the military," he says, rotating his shoulder. "There are boxing gloves for Mallet, a little crown for Kate." He laughs. "I had something else picked out for her, but she went with me to get this done and convinced the tattoo artist to substitute her thing out with a crown because she's a princess."

"She did not."

"Oh, she did. What she can get away with is amazing when she flutters her lashes at men. I don't get it." He sighs. "There's a baseball for Chase because he taught me how to throw a ball. Sometimes, I think he used it as an excuse to hit me and not get into trouble, but whatever."

"He wouldn't do that."

"Yes, he would." He shakes his head, pointing at a square. "That didn't come out great, but it's supposed to be a Lego to represent Gavin. We spent so many hours playing with Lego when we were kids."

I turn his arm to see the far side more clearly. "What is the last one? I can't see it from here."

"That one is a pumpkin."

My eyes widen as I try to sit up. He holds me against him, burying his face in my hair. I grip his arm and pull it to me until I can see the final item.

Yup. It's a pumpkin.

His voice from Thanksgiving, our first year together, echoes through my head. *"I'm just going to start calling you pumpkin since you like it so much."*

"Luke ..."

He nods, his heart pounding. Each beat taps the side of my face at the same tempo as my heart races in my chest.

I turn his arm back and forth to see if I missed any. *Is that it? Just his family and ... me?*

"Needless to say, I didn't expect you'd ever see that," he says, exhaling.

"When did you get your tattoo?"

"I don't know. Three or four years ago."

Three or four years ago?

"Is this weird or creepy?" he asks. "I'm not sure how I would take it if I were a woman and found out an ex-boyfriend got a tattoo to remind him of me years after we'd broken up. I didn't think about it at the time."

He tries to keep me from getting up again, but this time, I power through. I want to see his face, to take in those beautiful green eyes, and to treasure this moment.

The sheets pool at my waist as I twist to face him.

"Weird or creepy?" I ask, grinning. "Luke, I don't know what to think about this, but *weird* and *creepy* aren't two words I'm considering."

He lays a hand on my thigh. "I missed you. I missed you so fucking much. And when I was selecting something for everyone in my family, it wasn't complete until I added you to it." He grins. "Even if I never saw you again, and I didn't think I would at that point, you still belonged with me. To me, at least."

His words touch my heart as much as the pumpkin in the horseshoe. His genuineness blows me away. His honesty raises the bar to a level that no man will ever come close to reaching. All those nights, I sat alone in hotel rooms and tour buses, wondering if anyone was thinking about me beyond the show I just performed ... and Luke was getting a tattoo to keep me close.

Tears well in my eyes.

I don't think my own family would do something like this unless I paid them.

"I think it's special, lovely, sweet, and a million other things," I say, lacing his fingers through mine. "Do you ever wonder what would have happened if we would've figured things out? Are you ever curious where we might be?"

He studies our hands. "Yes and no." He brings our fingers to his lips and kisses them. "I think about it often. We'd probably have babies right now. Hopefully, a little girl who looks just like you and a little boy who loves horses as much as I do. We'd cook dinner together every night and watch documentaries while we go to sleep, and it would be so boring and absolutely perfect."

A single tear slides silently down my cheek.

"But you were destined for greatness, Laina. You were meant for something more than a little house in the middle of nowhere with a man who will never be able to give you all the things that you deserve. I really have nothing to offer you."

Oh, Luke. If you only understood that you're the only one who can offer what would make me happy... you.

That's it. That's why he didn't come for me.

He doesn't think he's enough.

Why would he think that?

Another tear spills over the edge and travels over my lips and down my chin. Luke brushes it away with the pad of his thumb.

Doesn't he understand that he's more than enough for me? Doesn't he see how good and honorable and respectable he is—and that my life is littered with snakes and rats and people ready to betray you for a check?

It's my life that's not good enough for him. And I hate that with every fiber of my being.

"Do you think we could make it work now?" I ask.

"I want to hear what you think."

My lungs fill with air. I exhale slowly, thinking about the men in my life—namely my father and Tom—the two men who were supposed to love and protect me.

I gave them everything I had to give: loyalty, honesty, and transparency. I communicated as clearly as I could. I showed them respect, even when they didn't deserve it, and gave them the benefit of the doubt more times than I can count. Yet they didn't reciprocate any of it.

The idea of adding another man to my life when I'm in the process of removing the only two currently taking space in the lineup is frightening—*except it's Luke*. It's not even like I'm adding him to my life because he's always been there. Even when I was devastated that we were done, he was always there.

After all, he was the only person I thought of when I desperately needed a safe place to land. *Him*. It's always been him.

I smile. "You are the only man I can imagine trusting enough to let into my life. You understand what loving someone means."

He grabs my other thigh and pulls me closer.

"You don't hide things from me, Luke. And I know you won't be manipulated by terrible stories in the media and the whispers that constantly surround me." I grin. "You're solid as hell."

"So, you do think we can make it work?"

"I think there's a lot to work out. I'm unsure what that looks like, and I know it won't be easy. But I know that I will either be alone forever or I will be with you."

He swallows. "You're sure?"

"No one else understands me. I don't think they can. You knew me before all this music stuff, and no one realizes *I'm still that girl*. Besides," I say, straddling him. "My heart belongs to you. You can take it or leave it."

"It would be really awkward if I said I wanted to leave it now that you're rubbing your pussy against my cock, huh?"

If I thought he was serious, I'd be humiliated. But there's no piece of his words or a single feature that isn't playful. That isn't full of love.

"See, that was my plan," I say, grinding myself against him. His cock hardens as my juices coat him. "I figured if you were going to turn me down, I'd make it really hard for you to resist me."

He grips my hips and lifts his to help the cause. "I'm still not sure how I'm going to respond. You better try harder."

I stop moving and pout. "Oh, darn."

He chuckles mischievously.

I lift high enough to grip his cock. It's thick in my hand—steel wrapped in velvet. Holding his gaze, I lower myself slowly onto him.

He hisses, his eyes squeezing closed as I take him in.

Once I'm fully seated, I slowly rock my hips in a circle. "Is this helping?"

"A little."

I laugh and grip the headboard. He cups my breasts, growling as I begin to bounce on his cock.

"I thought you needed a nap and a snack," I joke, clenching my pussy around him.

"What happened to the cold compress?"

"Come in me, then I'll sit in a cold bath."

His eyes fly open. "Fucking hell."

"*Right there,*" I say, sucking in a hasty breath. "Pound that spot."

He meets me move for move, gripping my tits so hard it stings. The added sensation amplifies the riot firing off inside me. *Fuck, I love this.*

The buildup climbs dizzyingly fast, and every cell in my body braces for the impact. My thighs shake. My core is so hot it's as if I'm swallowing fire. The top of my head might blow.

I'm ... so ... close ... "Fuck!"

"Ride me, baby," he says through clenched teeth. His hands find my hips again, and he moves me up and down. "Ride my dick all the way through it. Don't stop."

"I can't."

"Yes, you can." He thrusts into me from the bottom until his body goes taut. Then he begins to shake. "*Dammit.*"

I fight to open my eyes to watch him fall apart.

His head presses into the pillow, exposing his throat. A low, guttural sound escapes him. The tone scratches against my already sensitive skin, sending a second orgasmic wave tumbling through me.

I pant, my hands dropping to his chest. He wraps an arm around my waist and pulls me onto his chest. He struggles to catch his breath, too.

"You are quite the negotiator," he says, chuckling.

I laugh. "Does this mean you want to try to make it work?"

"This means I'm never letting you leave my life again."

I nestle against him. *Thank God for that.*

Chapter Seventeen

Luke

I pull out of my driveway, taking a right instead of a left. Troy answers before I pass my mailbox.

"Castelli."

"Hey, Troy."

"What can I do for you, Luke?"

"I'm running to the feed store. I'll be gone an hour, maybe. Just giving you a heads-up. Laina was doing the dishes when I left. If anyone shows up, you might just let her handle it. She's in a bit of a pissy mood."

Troy gives me one chuckle. *One.* It's the first time in ten days I've heard him do anything besides relay or accept information.

"Noted," he says. "Are you expecting anyone while you're gone?"

"Nope. And if Gavin shows up, tell him to get his ass back to work."

"I'll let you know if we have any problems."

My brows pull together. *Would he really say that to Gavin? I'm not sure. I think he might.*

"Well, all right," I say, wondering if I should mention that I was just joking. "Thanks."

The call ends.

My stomach knots like it does every time I talk to Troy. Guilt eats me alive for not telling Laina he's here. I've almost told her more than once; the truth was on the tip of my tongue. But then I remember Troy's insistence, and Anjelica's, that Laina's safety was on the line. And if she knew Troy was there, she might force him to leave.

I keep quiet.

I squint into the sun, driving a quarter mile before I can turn away from it. Luckily, I know where the giant pothole is in the center of the road and can swerve around it without seeing it.

"Laina, Laina, Laina," I say, exhaling. "What are you going to do, my lady?"

We've danced around reality for days. She's going to have to get back to her life soon. But it's not been brought up since the morning she rode me into submission.

I grin.

She knew my answer before she asked the question. She just played along.

The knot in my stomach pulls tighter.

Every time I think about this, I get nauseous. I don't know enough about her life and what it entails to predict the future. *How much time does she get off? How busy is she daily? Will her schedule allow her to come home with me, or will I need to make a lot of trips to different cities to see her?*

Can a relationship truly survive that?

I've stayed awake for a few hours every night, mulling over our options. The only option not on the table is ending things. If I must give up my business, I will. And I dread it's going to come to that.

Of course, I'd have an answer if I'd just come out and ask her. But I don't. Everyone in her life pressures her for shit, and I won't add to her stress. Besides, in the end, it doesn't matter. The result is the same.

That girl is mine.

My phone rings through the truck, and I click a button on the steering wheel to answer. "Hello?"

"Sounds like you're in the truck," Kate says. "Where are you going?"

"To the feed store."

"Oh, that sounds like a great time," she says, her tone full of sarcasm. "I haven't talked to you in a while, so I wanted to check in."

"Well, if you weren't traveling all the damn time for work, maybe we'd run into each other a little more."

She laughs.

"Where are you this week?" I ask.

"Albuquerque. You should come out here sometime. It's beautiful."

"We'll see."

"You sound like Dad. *We'll see*," she says in her best Lonnie Marshall impression. "Anyway, I was calling you because I can't ask Gavin. Well, I mean *I could* ask Gavin, but I'm not going to."

I pull next to the store and park.

"What are you not asking Gav?" I ask.

"I called Chase a couple of nights ago, but his hands were covered in oil or something. I don't know. Anyway, Kennedy answered his phone until he got cleaned up."

"Okay ..."

"And she told me Gavin borrowed some of her clothes for a sick girlfriend who couldn't leave his house."

Oh, shit.

"Kennedy said he was really weird about it, but she promised not to tell her dad. Or Megan. That, obviously, doesn't mean she can't tell me."

I wince. "I'm pretty sure the promise not to tell was supposed to include everyone, not just Chase and Megan."

"You do know what's going on," she says as if she just solved a riddle. "Come on. Tell me."

118

"It's nothing, Kate."

"It's something, Luke, or you'd tell me. And why is Gavin telling you secrets and not me? I didn't move home so you two could leave me out."

"You're just going to have to trust me on this one."

She huffs. "No. I won't. I refuse. Tell me, or I'm telling Chase."

I groan, wishing my niece wasn't a snitch. *We're going to talk about this. Later.*

I wish I could tell my sister what's going on. She might even be helpful. If Kate is good at anything, it's understanding women. But I swore to Laina that I wouldn't say anything, and I'm keeping my word.

"Please, Kate. It'll all come out soon." *I hope.* "But don't get anyone riled up over this. *Please.* Do it for me."

"For you, huh?" She hums. "What will I get out of not telling?"

"You'll be a good person."

"Overrated."

"*Kate ...*"

My sister laughs. "Fine. But you had better talk with Gavin, and the two of you had better start including me in stuff. I'm the baby of the family, remember. I can be a brat."

"You're always a brat."

"Okay. Go buy your horse things or whatever you're doing. I need to get back to work."

"Love you, Kate."

"Love you. Bye."

"Goodbye."

Chapter Eighteen

Laina

I dry my hands on a kitchen towel, side-eyeing my cell phone. I haven't had it out since I got it back a week ago. The disconnect from my life for the last ten days has been one of my life's greatest, most glorious periods.

No stress.

No bullshit.

No decisions to be made, meetings to attend, or events to prepare for so that someone else looks like Prince Charming.

Undoubtedly, there are important things to handle, media fallout to contend with, and many questions to answer from all directions. But I've been perfectly fine letting someone else, anyone else, deal with all of that. Except in the past few days, reality has begun gnawing away at me ... *in so many ways*.

Luke hasn't asked me when I might leave, but he knows it's coming. Staying indefinitely was never the plan. Then again, neither was falling in love with him again.

I was supposed to be on my honeymoon, so my calendar has been clear. But those days are dwindling, and my commitments are on the horizon ... and I don't know what that means.

Will we have a long-distance relationship? Can I cut back on my engagements to be here more? What will my security team say about me being here often?

I'm not even sure Luke locks his doors at night.

"We'll figure it out," I say, tossing the towel on the counter. "Trust the process." I eye my phone again. It's next to the coffee maker like a bomb ready to explode. *Fuck.* "Might as well get this over with."

I power it on and wait for it to load. The alerts ping as soon as it connects to the towers, or whatever phones do. And they ping. And they ping. And ping again.

I missed calls from nearly every contact in my phone—from acquaintances to friends to business partners. The number of texts awaiting me is ridiculous. *Maybe I'll need a new phone number because I can't handle that.*

Anjelica is at the top of the call list with a missed one from only a few minutes ago, so I touch her name and wait for it to ring. She picks up quickly.

"Anjelica Grace."

"Hi. It's Laina."

"Hey, how are you doing? Everything okay?"

"Yeah. I'm just trying to wean myself back into the real world."

"Probably a good idea. Did you see I called or is this a coincidence?"

No censure. No anger. No frustration. Anjelica was definitely the right person to call first.

I sit at the table. "I saw you called. Although I was going to call you anyway. What's up?"

"I've been working with public relations to keep a handle on things. The hubbub has started to die down. Well, it did start to die down, but your ex-fiancé decided to stoke the fire this morning."

The hairs on the back of my neck stand on end. "What do you mean?"

"Tom and your father were at a charity golf tournament this morning. According to *Exposé*, Tom was quoted as saying you got cold feet, and the wedding would likely happen privately."

He what?

I swallow down my parched throat. "What in the hell is he talking about?"

"That answers my question."

"Which was ...."

"If something had changed and you forgot to let us know."

I laugh angrily. "Anjelica, I assure you, I will not be marrying Tom Waverly anywhere at any time. *Ever.*" My hands shake. "And, of course, my father was standing right there, giving credence to Tom's bullshit. I can't ..."

I take a deep breath before I continue with my thoughts. Because if I do what I want, a tsunami will be left in its wake.

But the longer I sit with the idea of firing my father as my business manager and removing him from every part of my business, the more it makes sense.

The more urgent it feels.

How many times have I asked for a break? How many times has he executed a contract despite my insistence that I didn't want to be on a project? How often has he talked down to me and washed over concerns I raised about safety and money?

And now he's playing golf with Tom? In a charity golf tournament like either of them have a heart. When I refused to marry the asshole.

I hate them both so much.

It's not just the anger boiling inside me, though. I feel so .... betrayed. If Anjelica had said that my dad had reached out numerous times to make sure I was okay, I'd probably feel less unhinged now. *But, no.* He's playing golf with the man I just walked out on as if I just got cold feet.

How would he know? There certainly wasn't a missed call from him or Mom on my phone.

He doesn't care about me as a person, and he can fuck right off.

I'm done.

"Can we schedule a meeting as soon as I return to Nashville?" I ask.

"When are you getting back?"

My heart is heavy. "I'm not sure. I'll be there by the first of the week."

"Is Monday afternoon good? Say, around three?"

"Perfect."

"I'll add it to your calendar," she says. "But I have to ask—what do you want to talk about?"

My palm sweats against the phone. "I want to make some changes. I want to be more in control of my schedule. I want to see every contract and offer, and I don't want anyone to have the authority to sign on my behalf. Not right now."

"Am I hearing you correctly? You want to remove your father from your management team?"

"Yes," I say, ignoring the pit in my stomach. "That's precisely what I want. I want him off everything. Is that hard to do?"

"It's a lot of paperwork, and we need PR to be on the ball, ready to nip any negative press in the bud. How soon do you want to do this, Laina?"

"As soon as possible."

"Let me get with legal then and have them start the process." She sighs. "Can you hold on, please?"

"Sure."

The line shuffles for a few moments until I'm put on speakerphone.

"Laina, you're on speakerphone. Coy Mason is here."

"Hey, Laina. How are you?" he asks.

"I'm good, Coy. You?"

"I'm good. Thank you for asking."

"Laina," Anjelica says, "may I fill Coy in on our conversation?"

I nod. "Sure," I say without hesitation.

Coy Mason was the biggest name in country music until a couple of years ago. He still performs under his stage name, Kelvin McCoy, from time to time. But much of his effort is spent running Mason Music. For someone so big in the music world, Coy is as down-to-earth as they get. His boutique label quickly became one of the most powerful labels in music, and I'm honored to be one of their first recording artists.

"What's going on?" he asks.

"Laina is making a couple of management decisions, namely, firing her current manager."

Coy pauses. "Your father manages you right now, correct?"

"Yes."

He blows out a breath. "I won't act like this isn't tricky, and many emotions are involved when we work with family. Trust me. I see Boone every day."

I laugh.

He laughs, too. "How can we help you facilitate this? What do you need from us?"

"Coy, I don't even know. I've just pressed pause long enough to know that I can't keep doing things as they were. I need to build a team who cares about me."

"I absolutely agree," he says. "Do you have any thoughts about who you might bring on as your business manager?"

"No. I probably should have an idea before I fire my father, huh?"

"Not necessarily," Anjelica says.

"Actually, once you decide something like this, you're better off executing it immediately. I've seen stuff happen where people realize what's going down and intentionally try to sink the ship, so to speak."

My heartbeat begins to settle. "What will happen to everything he handled if I don't have a replacement?"

"I want you to hire someone you're comfortable with, obviously," Coy says. "But have you met Hollis Hudson?"

"The songwriter?"

"Yes," Coy says.

"No. I've just heard his name. Why?"

124

Anjelica gasps. "I didn't think of that."

"Hollis has been working with a few of our artists and doing one hell of a job," Coy says. "He's smart. Tough as nails for his clients. But a teddy bear under all that muscle. Every artist we've sent his way has had the same thing to say. He listens. He's a go-getter. And he respects their wishes."

I laugh. *Does that really exist?*

"I'd keep him in mind, if I were you," Coy says. "I'd be happy to set up a meeting. And I know he'd be thrilled to support you."

"Wow," I say, stunned.

I've admired Hollis Hudson for years. And if Coy believes we'd be a good fit, then how can I refuse to consider him? I want someone who listens to me, who'll fight for me, and who respects my wishes. Combine that with someone who knows the ins and outs of this business? *Yes, please.*

"If you think we'd work well together, then yes, I'd really appreciate a conversation," I say.

"Great. If you need anything, call me," Coy says. "But I gotta run. My wife is trying to make homemade jam today, of all things, and I promised her I'd be there to taste test them all." He laughs. "Today is supposed to be my day off, Laina."

"I see. Go have fun jam-tasting," I say, laughing.

A door shuts in the distance.

"He's always a wave of energy," Anjelica says, chuckling. "The man is brilliant, but it takes a lot to keep up with him."

"Sounds like it."

"All right. I'll get your attorneys to work, but you'll need to touch base with them before they'll do too much. And no one will be alerted until you give the signal. Then I'll set up a meeting between us on Monday, as we discussed, and I'll get Hollis on your calendar as early as possible next week. Does that sound good?"

"Perfect."

She pauses. "And Laina?"

"Yeah?"

"It makes me really proud that you're doing this. It's been a long time coming."

I sink back into the chair and grin. *Yes, it most certainly has.*

"I appreciate that, Anjelica. Thank you for having my back."

"Always. Talk soon."

"Goodbye."

I turn the phone off and take a deep breath.

"It makes me really proud that you're doing this. It's been a long time coming."

It makes me proud of me, too, Anjelica.

I can do this. I won't be alone. And I can move forward with far more control over my life. And my father? Time will tell if he loves me for me or for what I bring him. *Kudos. Wealth. Control.*

That's about to be taken away from you, Dad. I hope we survive the fallout.

I look out the window. *What a beautiful day.* I find Kennedy's boots and head to the barn. It's time to do some mucking. And then maybe later, when Luke gets home, it'll be time to do something that rhymes with that.

Chapter Nineteen

L uke

I burst out laughing. "What the hell is this?"

The barn is not only *clean* but it is also organized. *And I didn't do it.*

My chest warms as I glance back at the house and wonder if Laina did it. I can imagine her out here in Kennedy's pink boots with a pair of leggings and a tank top that leaves little to the imagination. She's as adorable as shit, and she has been helping me more willingly. *I only had to coax her with oral once yesterday.* But to imagine her out here on her own is wild.

And so fucking hot.

I leave everything from the feed store in my truck except the present I bought Laina. I'm almost to the porch before she throws open the door and waves.

"That trip took entirely too long," she says, wrapping her arms around my neck and kissing the hell out of me.

"I could get used to this."

I scoop an arm under her ass and lift. Her legs lock around my waist as she kisses me again.

"Did you clean the barn?" I ask, stepping inside and closing the door behind us with my foot.

Her eyes sparkle. "Do you like it?"

"No. I love it. That was so sweet. Thank you, Pumpkin."

She bites her lip. "Every time you call me that, I think of your tattoo, and then I want you to fuck me. It's automatic. Boom, boom, boom."

"Your wish is my command."

"No, actually, put me down." She unwinds herself from me. "I did something else, and it's fantastic. I think you're going to love it."

"Wow. You cleaned the barn and did something else? You're on fire today."

"It's been a good day. But also, your one-hour trip turned into four. I had time to kill. What happened?"

I hand her a pink shirt from the feed store. "First, I got you a present."

She unfolds it and then giggles. "They even make them in pink?"

"Hey, women are farmers, too."

"Well, I can't wait to wear this. Thank you for being so sweet to me."

I pour myself a glass of tea. "You're my lady. Of course, I have to be sweet to you."

She beams.

"What's this other surprise?" I ask, taking a sip. "Tell me it's lingerie."

She makes a face. "No. It's a cake."

I laugh. "A cake?"

"Hang on."

The garage door opens and then closes. Laina comes around the corner carrying a two-layer cake covered in chocolate icing. It tilts slightly to the side, despite her attempt at leveling it out with extra icing and cherries.

It's the cutest damn cake I've ever seen.

"I was going through a cookbook I found in the back of a drawer," she says.

I lift a brow, making her laugh.

"And this recipe looked delicious. You had all the stuff—major green flag right there, by the way—so I whipped it up like a professional baker."

I start to tease her about the last cake she made ... and burned. But I think she's actually quite proud of herself this time. There's no way in hell I'm diminishing that.

"What flavor is it?" I ask.

"You had a yellow cake mix, so I used that. But I put in a secret ingredient that's supposed to make it smoother and richer. Then I made the chocolate icing." She draws her finger around the edge of the cake plate, covering the tip in a thick layer of icing. "Here. Try it."

She offers it to me. I grab her wrist, then suck the icing off, nipping the tip of her finger with my teeth. It sends a line of fire straight to my cock. I don't know how I'm keeping up with her. She wants to fuck three or four times a day—I'm here for it. I'll never say no—but I wonder how long she can keep up that pace.

It'll be a fun experiment.

"That was very, *very* good," I say. "Do you know what you should do?"

"Take this to the bedroom and roll all over it and then make you lick it off me?"

I nod. "Scratch my idea. Let's do yours."

She giggles. "What was your idea?"

"Take that with us to Mom and Dad's tonight for dinner."

Her eyes grow wary as she sets the cake on the counter. "Your mom is an excellent cook."

"So? That cake is amazing. She'll love it."

"I don't know ..."

I pull her into a hug and kiss the top of her head. "Don't do anything you don't want to do. But I'm proud of you and your cake, and I want to show you off."

She looks up at me. The pride in her eyes melts my heart. "Really? Or are you screwing with me?"

"I only screw you in the bedroom."

Although, that's not true. We've screwed in the bathroom, the dining room, the living room, and the kitchen table ... Any room where clothes can be removed, they've been removed.

I press a long, lingering kiss to her lips. "I'm serious about the cake. Just think about it. If you don't want to take it, I'm happy to leave it here and eat the whole damn thing."

Please be good, or else I'm going to have to get very crafty with hiding pieces of cake.

I follow Laina into the living room. She waits for me to sit, then curls up in my lap. It's her favorite spot, it seems.

"Sorry for taking longer than I said I would today," I say, sweeping her hair off her shoulder. "Tucker—do you remember him? He owns a trucking company in town."

"I don't think I do."

"Anyway, he called and asked me to swing by. He wants to put a benefit together for Cotton. They were good buddies. Their farms are side by side."

"That's nice of him."

I nod, my chest tightening as I think of Cotton. "Tucker isn't much of an extrovert, so he asked me and Gavin to help him put it together."

"You're going to?"

"Of course. I've been thinking of ways to show him our support. But we can't just take food over there or go visit him since they've already left for Chicago."

She rests her head against my chest. "What's the plan?"

"Cotton started a community charity a long time ago that helps kids access horses. It's expensive, and stables aren't always close. Through his program, kids from Peachwood County can take lessons free at any participating stable. I think all the stables around here are involved." I smile. "It's his pride and joy. We're going to hold a fundraiser, so Cotton knows it will remain funded for a while. Who knows what'll happen to it once he's gone."

"What are you going to do?"

"What started as a simple idea has steamrolled into about ten," I say, chuckling. *Par for the fucking course for my family.* "I think we're going to organize a car show next month. All of Cotton's friends are old car collectors, so they'll be happy to participate, I'm sure. Gavin talked to The Wet Whistle, and they will donate all profits on the day of the car show to Cotton's family. Mom is organizing an auction. Dad and Chase are putting together a fishing tournament the next day since a lot of the car guys will still be in town. And I'm going to organize a tack sale. That'll bring in all the horse people from all over. Kennedy and Kate want to expand it to a community-wide garage sale. We'll see."

I stop when I notice Laina's body shaking softly.

"Hey," I say, nudging her.

She doesn't look up at me.

"Hey," I say again, peeling her away so I can see her face.

Tears stream down her pretty little cheeks, leaving black mascara trails behind. Her lips are pouty as they tremble.

"What's wrong?" I ask, confused. "What happened?"

"Why are you guys so damn nice?"

She starts crying again. This time, I try not to laugh.

"Oh, Laina," I say, pulling her against me again. "I have no idea why that makes you cry, but I'm sorry? I think? I guess."

"Don't be sorry. There's nothing to be sorry over. It just ... I'm a little emotional today."

"Do you want to talk about it?" I ask.

She sits quietly, sniffling every now and then. I don't push her to open up, but I just comfort her, letting her know I'm here.

Finally, she straightens up and pulls her hair back into a ponytail.

"When is all of this happening?" she asks.

"We're shooting for three weeks from this Saturday if we can get it all put together and get the word spread fast enough."

"Well, I can help with that."

My brows pull together. "How?"

"I don't want to announce it quite yet because I might have to move some things around. I don't know. But I want to help. Would there be room for me to put together some kind of a concert?"

I'm stunned. My jaw hangs open, and I stare at her. *Is she serious?*

"Maybe we can rent the college football stadium in Fairwood," she says. "It's half an hour from here, but we could do it on Friday and advertise the Saturday activities. Or do it on Sunday and hopefully bring people to town on Saturday. I could do two concerts, one in the morning and one in the evening. I'll pay for security and the insurance, refreshments. Whatever we make, we donate to your friend."

The center of my chest burns. I press a palm to my forehead and stare at her, speechless.

"I just want to do something," she says. "My name has been used to draw attention to a lot of rich people and inconsequential bullshit. I'm just ... I'm over it. I'm taking control like I should've a long time ago. What better place to start than to help the community I grew up in?"

"Laina, I don't know what to say. This is an incredible offer."

She kisses me softly. "Don't say anything. This kind of thing is long overdue."

I wrap her in my arms and rock her back and forth. *I love you so fucking much.*

The words are on my tongue, ready to slip into the air and world. But I'm not sure if she's ready to hear them yet.

My life has been so lonely, so incomplete, without her. I can see that now. I've survived but barely lived. I've worked hard and built my business, and I've had fun with my family. I've even gone on dates. *But this? Having Laina in my house to welcome me home, to be eager for me to get here?* There's absolutely nothing better. I'm sure of it.

We have to be at Mom's in two hours, and I need a shower and a shave. But I can't convince myself to get up with her in my lap.

This is what I always imagined it would feel like to have Laina here. Warm and full ... *like a home.*

"I fired my dad today," she whispers.

I flinch. "What?"

"It's true. I called Anjelica and talked to her and Coy, and they're getting the ball rolling. Coy has someone who might be a good fit for me to meet with next week. Regardless, I'm no longer having my father involved in my business."

Oh fuck. I lace my fingers together at her chest. "Did something happen? Or is this just something that needed to be done?"

"Both." She takes a deep breath. "I'm tired of everyone making decisions for me like I'm a child that can't possibly know what's best for herself. And I heard that Tom and my father were at a golf thing together."

I bristle at the information.

How could her dad be in the same room with Tom Waverly? I don't give a shit that he's a powerful movie star. Tom obviously hurt his daughter. How is he not throwing punches, let alone playing golf with the fucker?

"It gets worse, if you can imagine that," she says, her body going rigid. "A reporter apparently brought up the wedding, and Tom, with my dad standing right there, said we decided to do something more intimate. That I just got cold feet."

I take a breath to keep myself from exploding.

"Are you mad?" she asks.

"I'm pissed."

Her head falls forward. "I'm sorry. I had no idea, or I would've warned you, and I never imagined he would—"

"*Whoa,*" I say, twisting her until she's facing me. I hold her face in my hands. "What are you doing?"

"I'm apologizing."

"For what?" I kiss her forehead. "Don't apologize for other people's bullshit. I know you had nothing to do with that."

Her eyes widen. "You do?"

"Of course, I do. What did you think? That I'd believe a punk that's bitter that his beautiful girl realized what a clown he is and left him?" I tap her on the nose. "*Come on.* You know I'm smarter than that."

Relief melts off her. The worry is replaced with a sly smile.

"How much time do we have before we have to go to your mom's?" she asks.

"A couple of hours. Why?"

"I know a way you can kill an hour." She hops to the floor. "What did we decide to do with that cake?"

My balls tighten. "It's up to you."

"I'll bake your mom another one. This one is tilted anyway."

She scoots into the kitchen, leaving me laughing behind.

God, I love this woman.

I really, really do.

Chapter Twenty

Laina

"What in the almighty is happening?" Maggie Marshall clutches her chest, her jaw hanging on the floor. "Laina Kelley. Is that you, honey?"

I shrug, giggling. "It's me. Ta-da!"

"What? *Luke*? What the ... Oh, the hell with it." She rushes toward me with her arms spread wide. "Get over here and hug an old woman, will ya?"

Luke laughs as Maggie all but envelops me in her arms.

"Lonnie, get in here," she shouts, nearly taking out my eardrums. "We have company!"

"It is so good to see you, sweetheart," she says, pulling away. Her eyes are the same color as Luke's. "Let me get a look at you. You're just as pretty as a picture."

"It's good to see you, too, Maggie. How have you been?"

"I've been wonderful. Kate moved back, Chase got married, and you are here." She laughs in disbelief. "Why didn't someone tell me you were still in town?"

My stomach twists, and I look at Luke. I'm not sure what to say. *Do I bring up the wedding fiasco? Or do we slide over it and pretend it didn't happen?* This would've been a great thing to consider before we were in the moment.

"No," Maggie says, smacking my arms. "Don't do that."

"Don't do what?" I ask, my nerves bouncing around like kangaroos.

She glances at Luke, then at me. "I'm going to take the blanket off the baby. Or I should really say *take the veil off the bride.*" She waits for a reaction, but I'm unsure what to give her. "It's a joke. I was kidding."

"Too soon, Mom. Too soon," Luke says.

"Anyway," Maggie says, "all joking aside, we're not going to dance around what happened. You were supposed to get married. You didn't. It happens to a lot of people. Now let's move on."

My shoulders sag. I'm so relieved that I could cry.

"What are you hollerin' about in here?" Lonnie asks, coming into the room. He stops in his tracks when he sees me. "Aren't you a sight for sore eyes?"

"Hi, Lonnie," I say, grinning.

He comes to me and pulls me in for a one-arm hug. "How have you been, sweetheart?"

"I'm good. What about you?"

"Oh, I'm doing about the same as I always am. Taking orders from Maggie and Kate and shoving off what I can on my boys."

"Ain't that the truth," Luke mumbles.

Maggie rolls her eyes. "I'm embarrassed that I made a meatloaf for dinner."

"Why would that embarrass you?" I ask.

"Because you're here. I need to woo you so you come back more often." She motions for me to follow her. "Now, come in here and help me mash these potatoes."

My heart is so full it nearly overflows.

It feels so good to be among these people and treated like any other person in the world. I'm instructed to mash the potatoes and corrected when I don't add enough salt. I'm quizzed not on which celebrities I've seen lately or about the songs on my albums but on if I take vitamins and what books I've read.

Refreshing doesn't begin to cut it. This is ... wholesome. There's no guilt for hurting their son. No anger for not calling. No snide comments to make me feel like a jerk. All that's here is love and forgiveness. It's family.

It's a home.

"Rinse that hand mixer off and put it in that drawer over there," Maggie says, pointing across the kitchen.

"Careful," Luke says. "She'll go through every drawer in here."

"Oh, I will not. I only go through *your* drawers," I say, smiling at him.

"You didn't find my new set of lures, did ya?" Lonnie asks.

Luke groans. "I told you I didn't take them."

"Then who did?"

"Not me, Dad. Probably that little shit of a granddaughter," Luke says, grinning.

"I'm telling Kennedy you said that," Maggie says, shoving spoons into the potatoes and green beans. "Gavin will be her favorite uncle. You know how much you hate battling back into first place."

I laugh. "What are you talking about?"

"Guys, come fix your plates," Maggie says before turning to me. "Gavin and Luke have a little competition going with Kennedy. It's been going since she was old enough to know how to manipulate them. Poor boys. Anyway, she keeps a leaderboard of which uncle is her favorite. Gavin and Luke always try to stay on top."

"Oh," I say. "I see."

"Here." Maggie shoves a plate in my hand. "Eat up. I'm sorry that it's just meatloaf."

"Maggie, I haven't had a home-cooked meal like this in forever."

Luke's hand slips across my lower back as he passes by. Goose bumps break out across my skin.

"If you need a home-cooked meal, just call me," she says, pouring us all a glass of tea and taking it to the table. "I used to send Kate food all the time. I'm a pro. Send me a menu and I'll have it to you the next morning."

"She spoils those kids rotten," Lonnie whispers loud enough for everyone to hear.

"Not me," Luke says, putting potatoes on my plate and then his. "I'm the middle child. I get overlooked."

Maggie sighs. "Now that's an outright lie. Anytime I try to ignore you, you borrow my car and don't bring it back, so I have to call. Or you fill my washing machine with your laundry and forget to start it. Or you—"

"We get the picture, Mother," Luke says. "You love my brothers more than me. Got it."

I smile at Maggie as we make our way to the table. She shakes her head at Luke.

"Why do you do this to me?" she asks him. "Why do you make me think you just might really believe that, so I'll worry about it when I go to bed tonight?"

"I'm sorry," Luke says as the four of us settle at the table. "I didn't know you stayed up worrying like that. I'll make sure you know I'm kidding before I leave or hang up. Promise."

"Or just don't drive me crazy on purpose."

"Unlikely."

We eat quietly, enjoying each other's presence and the delicious food. I compliment Maggie on her cooking. She beams. I wish it were that easy to make everyone happy.

"Luke, what's on the side of your head?" Lonnie asks. "Bend over here. Is that mud?"

I press my lips together and refuse to make eye contact with Luke.

"It's nothing," Luke says, his face heating before our eyes.

"Yeah, it is. Hold still." Lonnie plucks a chunk of chocolate icing from Luke's hair. "What is this? Candy?"

He chokes on a green bean. "Yeah, Dad. It's candy."

"How do you get candy in your hair?" Maggie asks, shaking her head. "You never cease to amaze me, Lucas."

"He never ceases to amaze me either," I say.

I look at him at the exact moment he looks at me. He'd be balls deep inside me if we weren't at his parents' kitchen table and they weren't sitting beside us. There is no doubt.

"How are your parents, Laina?" Lonnie asks.

I clear my throat. "They're doing well."

"Where are they living these days?"

"Los Angeles. They moved out there two or three years ago, I think."

Maggie slices her meatloaf. "Please tell them we asked about them."

Lonnie chews slowly, his brows tugged together like Luke's when he's thinking.

I set my fork down. "I'm going to be honest with you. I very rarely talk to my parents. I haven't been to their home in LA, and they didn't see me for the holidays last year."

Maggie sets her fork down, too. "Oh, honey. Why not?"

"Because they're assholes," Luke says, firing his father a look I can't quite read.

"*But she's their child,*" Maggie says to her son. "Are you okay, sweetheart?"

I know this must be unbelievable to Maggie and Lonnie, two people who love their children more than their own lives. They must think there's something wrong with me not having a relationship with my parents. But it's the truth, and I don't want to hide it from them.

I'm tired of hiding from the things that make me uncomfortable.

Luke reaches for my hand under the table, squeezing it tightly.

"So," Maggie says, reading the room. "How did the two of you see one another again?"

"Laina needed a place to stay away from the paparazzi, and my house was the perfect answer," Luke says.

I smile at him. *Thank you for not telling them I broke into your house without asking you first.*

He winks at me.

"Well, I, for one, am glad you are here," Lonnie says. "We've missed you. I know Luke has missed you. He was devastated when he came back from seeing you in Cleveland."

Seeing me in Cleveland?

Luke's face pales.

"I'm sorry," I say, focusing on Lonnie. "When Luke visited me in Cleveland?"

"Does anyone need more potatoes?" Maggie asks. "Or tea? I'm getting up and can bring it back."

No one says a word.

Lonnie stabs a chunk of meatloaf and lifts his gaze to mine. "Yeah. Right after you left that last time. Luke got a ticket to see you in Cleveland, and then you guys broke up for good."

Luke didn't visit me in Cleveland. What's he talking about?

I would chalk it up to Lonnie having misunderstood a story or mixing up something that happened with one of his other children with Luke. But the guilt on Luke's face makes it clear.

He came to see me in Cleveland?

A million questions roll through my mind, and I try to sort them while conversing with Maggie.

"Right after you left the last time. Luke got a ticket to see you in Cleveland, and then you guys broke up for good."

That's not what happened. That's not *close* to what happened, so why would Luke tell them that?

He slides his hand from mine and places it on his lap.

I couldn't come home, and he didn't return my calls. That's what happened. Unless ...

Unless he did go to Cleveland.

I smile politely at Maggie as she sits with her tea, launching into a how-to on making lasagna. *Where did this come from? Did I miss something?* I want to tell her I don't care how to make anything right now. I want to know why Luke is lying.

There could be a reasonable explanation for it. Maybe he told his parents he was coming to see me, and he and Gavin went partying instead. But Lonnie was so sure. And Luke won't even look at me.

What am I missing?

"Does anyone want dessert?" Maggie asks, getting up to make her and Lonnie a cup of coffee. "Had I known you were coming, Laina, I would've made you a cheesecake. Do you still like those? With the chocolate on top?"

"How did you remember that?" I ask, grinning.

"You were here for years. A mother remembers."

The good ones do, Maggie. Not mine.

"I have brownies I can heat with ice cream," she says. "Or if you want to stay a little while, I'll whip up some chocolate chip cookies."

Luke finally looks at me. He shifts in his seat like he can't sit still. This time, it's not because he wants to devour me. This time, I think he wants to avoid me.

I'm not sure whether to be angry or nervous. It's the worst position to be in—there's no way to prepare. My body falls back into what it knows about situations like this and starts building a shield around my heart to protect it.

I hate it. I don't want to feel like this with Luke. I want the open, vulnerable, honest relationship we share. I want the chocolate cake and old sheets, the cuddles in the middle of the night, the horse barn antics during the day.

I don't want secrets, and I especially don't want secrets that make me feel like the odd man out.

"We're gonna go, I think," Luke says.

I stand and collect my dishes. "Let me stay and help you clean up."

"No, absolutely not," Maggie says. "I'll make Lonnie help me load the dishwasher."

He gives us an unenthusiastic thumbs-up. Despite my mood, I can't help but laugh.

"Are you sure?" I ask. "It's so rude to leave a house with dirty dishes."

"Go." She pulls me in for a quick hug. "And don't be a stranger. You're always welcome, of course, but if you can give me a heads-up next time, I'll make you something good."

"Dinner was great," I say. "Thank you for having me."

"Good night, Mom. Night, Dad," Luke says.

"Good night, son. Love you," Lonnie says. "It was good to see you, Laina."

"It was good to see you, too. Good night."

My insides twist so tightly that I think I might hurl as we step into the night.

Chapter Twenty-One

Laina

Luke doesn't say a word on the walk to the truck. He opens my door, waits for me to get situated, and then shuts me inside.

I don't know how to bring this up to him. I don't want to sound accusatory, like he lied to his parents. But he was lying to them, *or he's been lying to me.*

For the life of me, I can't figure out why this is a thing. *How can I possibly be caught up in another situation that affects me and I'm totally in the dark?*

Why does this keep happening?

Luke climbs in and starts the truck. He doesn't look at me as he puts it in reverse and backs down the driveway. We hit the road under the cover of darkness, God forbid anyone see me and give me something else to worry about tonight, and head toward his house.

The longer we travel silently, the more time I have to think. It's uncanny how similar it is to situations with my father when he refuses to explain why everyone around me knows something *about me* that I don't.

And I also can't avoid comparing when I sat with Tom, waiting for an explanation about the Paris photos. Nothing was satisfactory that time either.

My cheeks flush. My chest tightens. I can't help but be self-conscious, *and I hate it.*

We're halfway there before I can't take it anymore. If I let him, he'll clearly avoid the discussion. Too bad for him—I won't.

"What was that back there?" I ask, trying to sound normal and not on the verge of coming out of my skin.

"What do you mean?"

I laugh, the sound tight and twisted. "Please don't act like I'm a fool."

"I'm not. Or I don't mean to."

"Then answer me."

"Why are you so upset?" he asks.

My eyes widen. "Short answer? I have trust issues."

"And you don't trust *me?*"

I don't want to be mad at him. I really, *really* don't. But the more he dances around the question, the harder it is to stay *not* mad.

"It's weird," I say, watching his profile. "I do trust you. You're one of the few people in this world I trust, and you know this. You know the shit I've gone through with people being shady."

He regrips the steering wheel.

"So imagine my surprise when your dad says you came to see me in Cleveland like it's a fact. Only, the thing is that I was there, and you, Luke, were not."

I pause, allowing him to jump in, but he doesn't take the opportunity.

"What am I supposed to think?" I ask. "That you lied to your dad? Or did you lie to me? Or is this all a huge misunderstanding, and you're just acting odd for fun? Because that, your failure to come to Cleveland—or anywhere, really—is what broke us apart."

He whips his head to mine. "You want to pin that all on me?"

"I called you. You didn't answer or call me back. I couldn't jump on a plane and come home to you, and you knew that. Anyone in their right mind who wanted to save a relationship would've tried, and you, Luke Marshall, didn't." I heave a breath. "I'm not even mad about that. I don't want to get sidetracked. I just want to know what you're hiding from me."

My chest is so tight that it's hard to breathe. Each breath is shaky. I don't know whether to yell or cry, but I'm scared, and my emotions are building.

And I've put my trust in him. *Please don't break it.*

"Okay," he says, turning onto his road. "I did fly to Cleveland to see you."

My jaw drops.

"You were amazing, Laina," he says, shaking his head like he's reliving the experience. "I'd never seen anything like it. You owned the stage and every person in attendance. It was incredible." He looks at me. "*You* were incredible."

Tears flood my eyes.

"I was so fucking proud of you," he says, smiling sadly. "I was a fanboy in the crowd, wanting to tell everyone you were my girl. But I knew they wouldn't believe me. Look at you ... and look at me."

"Why didn't you tell me you were there? I don't understand."

"I didn't tell you I was coming because I wanted to surprise you. I had this big, stupid idea that I would find you after the show and tell you that I couldn't live without you and that we'd figure out how to make things work."

I cover my mouth with my hand.

He did come for me.

Luke lowers the speed as we hit the gravel and takes the bend slowly.

The sky is jet-black and starless. This far from town, there are no streetlights, and the only thing you can see is wherever the headlights shine. It seems fitting.

"It has killed me to hear you say that I didn't come for you—that I didn't fight for us," he says, pulling up the driveway. "Because I did go to you. I did try to make things right. My God, it's all I ever wanted."

"Then why didn't you see me?"

We climb to the top of the hill. He parks the truck and then kills the engine.

"I called you after the concert," he says warily. "Your dad answered your phone."

My spirits sink. A bitter taste rises from my stomach, and I nearly gag.

"He had me come backstage." Luke stares at the house—not at me. "So I did. Your dad met me at a certain place, and I knew immediately something was wrong. He led me down a hallway and then cracked open a door." A faint smile settles on his lips. "You were sitting on a couch with a handful of girls and guys living the dream. You looked so happy. I couldn't take that away from you."

I swallow past a lump in my throat. "But I wasn't happy, Luke. I was playing a part. When you're on stage performing, you're not Laina Kelley, the girl from Indiana who used to have a lemonade stand every summer and charged fifty cents a cup. You become someone else, a caricature, almost. That stadium full of screaming fans? They're not there to support *me*. They're there to sell the Laina Kelley, the woman who never has bad days. The one who always smiles. The one with the perfectly curated answer to every question because no one is allowed to ask her questions unless they're submitted beforehand and cleared."

Irritation gets the best of me, and I get out of the truck.

"Why are you mad?" he asks, meeting me at the porch.

"Because ..." I calm myself. I don't want to make this worse. I don't want to blow it up into something I'll regret in the morning. "You realize you stripped me of being happy, right?"

"I wasn't happy either."

"But you decided that for yourself. You're allowed to do that. But why does every fucking person in my life think I can't decide those things for myself?"

My voice is entirely too loud for the conversation, but it's get loud or cry.

"Just to be clear," he says, narrowing his eyes. "I didn't break my own damn heart to hurt you. I was young. Naive. Foolish. What do you want me to say? When your dad told me that you were contemplating a world tour but wouldn't do it if I came back into your life—"

"*What?*"

Luke takes a step back.

"You and my father discussed what you thought was best for me?" I ask so calmly that Luke puts even more space between us. *Smart man.* "Oh, my gosh. You had your own little clandestine deal going behind the scenes, and I didn't even know."

"Laina—"

"Why am I surprised?" I laugh at myself. "Why did I think that you were above that? Because I did. I didn't think there was a chance in hell that you would team up with my father—"

"That's not what happened."

I square my shoulders to his. "Did you or did you not have a conversation with him in which the sole purpose was to decide my future?"

He looks at the ground.

"Dammit, Luke. Why does everyone think they get to speak for me? Think for me? Why does everyone assume that someone else can handle me better than I can handle myself?"

"It wasn't like that, Laina. Not for me." He whips his face to mine, his eyes blazing. "Please listen to me for a second."

"Why have you never told me this? Why did I have to hear it from your dad?"

"I started to tell you a hundred times, but I didn't want to add fuel to the fire."

I pace a circle, trying to relieve some of the energy looking for an escape.

"There were so many days, weeks, and even months when I dissected everything about myself," I say. "You were my best friend, my confidant. And I was in this new and exciting world and just wanted you with me. I needed you, Luke."

"I'm sorry."

"I had a new experience and wanted to share it with you every day. And so many times, I was lonely and scared, holed up in a hotel room with no one to talk to. And I called you, and you didn't answer."

"I live with that regret every day of my life."

"It's even more than that. I wanted to share your wins and be there for you when you needed me. I wanted to hear about your job and listen to your stories. Gosh, I missed your stories. And you just ripped it away from me because someone told you to?"

I scrub my face with my hands, wishing we hadn't gone to Maggie's. I hate that I didn't know any of this. That, once again, I was ignored. My feelings, my heart was ignored. *These men are supposed to love me. Not crush me.*

"What else is there I don't know? Are there more secrets swimming around out there that someone decided I didn't need to know?"

His jaw sets. "Yeah. There is."

I was only kidding. I was being a dick. I didn't expect there to be more.

"Troy Castelli has been here since you arrived," Luke deadpans.

"You have to be fucking kidding me."

"He showed up the next morning and told me your label dispatched him. He said there were threats to your life, ones you may not take seriously, so I shouldn't tell you."

I gasp. "You're one of them."

"What?"

"*You.* You're just one of them."

He laughs menacingly. "You know what? You're going too far. I

148

understand you're pissed, but *do not* act like I'm out to hurt you. That's not fair."

"You wanna know what's not fair?"

"I know, I know," he says, his voice carrying on the wind. "Why don't you stop for one minute and think this through? I know people have put you through some shit, Laina. I'm sorry for that. I'm sorry for not being there for you. You have absolutely no idea what I'd do to go back and change it. To realize then the games being played that I was too naive even to comprehend." He takes a step toward me. "*But I can't, and I wasn't.*"

I battle tears from falling down my cheeks.

"You've been treated so badly by everyone that you expect it," he says, shaking his head in disbelief. "You know me, Laina. You know how much I fucking love you. You know my heart. Yet when things get hard, *you expect me to hurt you.*"

Hot, salty rivers flow down my face because he's right. I expect everyone to hurt me ... including him.

It's not right. I know that. I wish to hell that I didn't feel this way. But I'm afraid to stop expecting it because what happens when I'm unprepared?

I'll be crushed.

And I'm the only one I can trust to keep me from being crushed.

He levels his gaze with mine. "I would never hurt you. Not on purpose. And every decision I made was to save you pain. Do you think boarding the flight home from Cleveland was easy without you? It was one of the worst days of my life. But I did it. I broke my heart because I believed it would save yours."

We stand under the dark sky not as a couple but as two injured hearts shielding ourselves from the other.

"Let's go inside and get some rest," he says, dejected. "We can figure this out tomorrow."

"I'll take the couch."

He shakes his head and takes the stairs. "Take the bed. I'm not going to sleep anyway."

Instead of going to the sofa, he goes right into the kitchen and out the back door. I watch as the light comes on in the barn, and he doesn't return.

I go upstairs and cry myself to sleep.

It won't be the first time.

It probably won't be the last.

Chapter Twenty-Two

L uke

I print out the last two invoices and stick them in the pile on the corner of my desk. They need envelopes and stamps because I can't figure out how to bill customers electronically. Most of them are older and wouldn't know what to do with an e-invoice, anyway. Although I'm out here for a distraction and have been for the past two hours, I don't have the gumption to deal with the envelopes.

My heart fucking hurts.

I hate that she thinks I'd hurt her on purpose.

I can't stand that she's been through so much that her natural reaction is to assume the worst.

I wish to God that I wouldn't have left that stadium without seeing her that night, but I promise the man upstairs that I won't make the same mistake twice if he'll help me show her how much I love her.

Who can I talk to about this? Gavin would look for a quick fix. Mallet is still pissy about his divorce, so his advice would be question-able at best. I don't have the energy for Kate the Romantic, and

Chase ... Chase might actually be a good candidate. He has a wife. Somehow. He's usually a jerk, so he won't suggest courses of action full of fluff. He doesn't give a shit about anyone's feelings unless their names are Megan or Kennedy.

I find my phone under a paper plate and scroll to our family chat. A quick check of the time says it's too late to text my siblings, but that's what they get for having me as a brother.

> Me: Anyone up?

> Kate: Meeeee! What's cookin', good-lookin'?

> Me: Are you drinking?

> Kate: <laughing emoji> No, but I am delirious.

> Gavin: Hi, Kate.

> Kate: Not talking to you, Gav.

> Gavin: It's not my fault. I told you that.

> Me: It's absolutely his fault.

> Gavin: EXCUSE ME?

I can't help but smile.

Mallet: Is someone dead?

Kate: Not yet. I'm working on it. Wanna help?

Mallet: I have my own list of candidates. I'll help you if you help me.

Kate: Deal.

Me: How's training going, Mallet?

Mallet: Hard as fuck. What's going on back there?

Gavin: Why are you being so nice, Mallet?

Gavin: Is this actually Mallet?

Gavin: I think someone stole his phone.

Kate: You're pushing it, Gav.

I kick my boots up on my desk and lean back in my chair.

Me: I started this convo, and no one is talking to me.

Mallet: Typical middle child syndrome.

Kate: So why is everyone up this late? Is it a full moon or something?

Me: I'm looking at the sky right now, and it's black. No moon. Is that a moon phase?

Gavin: This convo is getting boring.

Mallet: Why? Because something halfway intelligent was just brought up?

I snort.

> Gavin: Tell your next opponent that I'll tell him how to kick your ass for free.

> Mallet: Better grow up, little boy, before you try to play with the men.

> Kate: STOP. Hell. Why did God give me all brothers?

> Me: Oh, like you'd survive with a sister.

> Mallet: She has one. Gavin.

> Gavin: Asshole.

I lean backward so I can see out the barn doors to check the house again. There are still no lights, no movement, just like it's been all night.

My fingers itch to touch her, and my arms beg to hold her. But it's late at night, and she's had a long, emotionally draining day. She fired her father, for fuck's sake, and then heard my bullshit.

Her words completely gutted me.

"There were so many days, weeks, and even months when I dissected everything about myself. I had a new experience and wanted to share it with you every day. And so many times, I was lonely and scared, holed up in a hotel room with no one to talk to. And I called you, and you didn't answer."

She'd been scared and lonely? Had no one to talk to? And I hadn't been there?

It makes it even more fucking amazing that she walked in here almost two weeks ago like she owned the place. She should have hated me for thinking I abandoned her.

I hate myself.

Not only that but growing up with my dad led me to believe that

I should trust her father. It never occurred to me that the man was a snake. How fucking wrong I was. No wonder she has trust issues. I need to do better. *I have to.* I have to take care of my girl.

Surely, she'll see that side of things in the morning. *Please, God.*

"It'll all be better in the morning," I say. "I just need to give her some space."

Me: I need some advice tomorrow.

Mallet: I'm busy.

I laugh.

Gavin: I'm GREAT at that. Call me.

Kate: If it has anything to do with a girl, call me.

Chase: I don't know why you fuckers think it's acceptable to blow up my phone at two in the morning, but you can fuck right off.

Me: I need advice tomorrow, Chase. Can I come over?

Chase: No.

Me: How does ten o'clock work?

Chase: I'm turning my phone off.

Kate: Night.

I stand and switch the light off on my desk.

Me: Going to bed, too.

Kate: Love you, Lukie.

Gav: Night.

Mallet: See ya.

I slip my phone into my pocket and head to the house.

Chapter Twenty-Three

Laina

I have an emotional hangover.

My body feels like I've run a mile, and my face gives me an idea of what it might be like to be in a street fight. Puffy eyes. Blotchy skin. A scowl that runs deep.

I'm in no mood for bullshit, yet I've caused my fair share of it recently. I lay awake in bed for most of the night and replayed everything Luke said.

"You know how much I fucking love you. You know my heart. Yet when things get hard, you expect me to hurt you."

The look on his face when he spoke those words is imprinted in my brain. I hate myself for making him feel that way.

He was right when he said my instinct is to assume the worst. That's such a shitty thing to do to other people, and it's an even shittier thing to do to myself.

Luke's note is on the kitchen table, telling me he was running to Chase's and that we would talk when he gets back. He signed it with an *I love you*, which has to be a good sign.

157

I want so badly for it to be a good sign.

We need to talk. We need to stop ignoring the writing on the wall and pretending we can live in this bubble for the rest of our lives. *Because we can't.* Our relationship will have complications, especially under the circumstances, and we need to work them out.

I need to stop punishing Luke for other people's sins.

Hopefully, he will forgive me for my knee-jerk reaction. He didn't deserve to be placed in the same basket as my dad and Tom.

I make a second cup of coffee and sit at the table with my phone. It finally powers on after charging all night. The pings begin immediately. I want to turn it back off, but I have to pull myself back to the land of the living. *To the land of reality.*

My inbox is a sea of unread messages. The sheer volume makes me anxious, but I'm determined to go through them. It's the only way to know what's going on in my business—especially now that I don't have a business manager.

I take a sip of my coffee when my phone rings. I touch the screen to decline it, but my finger slips against the green one first.

Fuck.

"Hello?" I say, tapping the speakerphone.

Please be a wrong number.

"Are you finally going to answer your damn phone?" My dad's voice freezes me in place. It's hostile. Ice-cold. *Furious.* "What the hell are you doing, Laina?"

"I'll get your attorneys to work, but you'll need to touch base with them before they'll do too much. And no one will be alerted until you give the signal."

Surely, Anjelica didn't tell him my plans ...

"I just got off the fucking phone with my attorney, and do you know what he said?" Dad booms. "He said that you were firing me as your business manager?"

Oh fuck.

I don't know how to respond, and I don't know what to say. I thought I had time to put together a response before he found out.

"Is that true?" He laughs hatefully. "Are you going to try to pretend to be a big girl and take care of every facet of your business—the one that I built from the ground up? You don't have a fucking clue where to start. And do you think anyone is going to do business with you after you just humiliated yourself with that farce of a wedding?"

Today is your lucky day.

I already know someone who wants to work with me. And I've heard from two good men, *men I respect*, that my actions showed bravery and wisdom.

"Maybe if you would've learned how to talk to me with the slightest bit of respect, we could've worked something out," I say. "But you sealed the deal when you played golf with Tom, and he gave that asshole statement about us still getting married. What the hell was that?"

"That was called keeping you from destroying your life."

"No, Dad, I think that was called covering your own ass."

"I'm trying to keep your options open, Laina. It's taken everything I can manage to get Tom even to consider talking to you again after you humiliated him in front of the whole world."

I laugh. "Why would you do that? I *don't* want to talk to him."

"*Don't be ridiculous.*"

"It's not your problem anymore. You're not on my payroll, and it sure as hell isn't like you act like my father."

"Do not talk to me that way."

I spring to my feet. "No, how about *you* don't talk to *me* this way. How about you don't talk to me at all. Your loyalties lie elsewhere, and that's fine. But keep them over there."

"You can't just fire me. I built that damn company."

"That's funny. The papers to terminate your employment are already in the works."

I can feel his anger pulsing through the telephone. "Listen to me, you ungrateful, entitled little bitch. I've put too much time and energy and money into this thing for you to drop me off on the side of the road like I'm disposable."

Ungrateful, entitled little bitch? That's how my father sees me? Oh, fuck that.

"Do you want to know what's hilarious?" I pace the floor. "It's hilarious that you think that I owe you anything. You've taken from me in every way. Financially. Emotionally. You've stolen my energy and almost worked me to death. You've depleted me in every way so you can get ahead in life. This happens to people every day, and most people aren't in a position to do something about it. *But I am.* Kick rocks, asshole."

"You realize that your business was built by me, right?"

"How? Because without me, *there is no business. I* write the music. *I* record the songs. *I* sell the albums, and *I* sell out the stadiums and sell the merch. So *my* business was built by me. Whatever you've taken from me—"

"Taken from you? How dare you insinuate that I've taken anything from you!"

I laugh in his ear. *Don't mind if I do.* "Did you think I wouldn't find out about the bonus you paid yourself at the end of the first quarter? Five million is a little excessive, don't you think? I called accounting this morning and am having a forensic audit performed by a third party. You better hope to God you aren't as fucked up as I think you are."

"If you pull this stunt, you can kiss your mother and me goodbye forever."

I wait for the tears to cloud my vision and the pinch to squeeze over the bridge of my nose. I swallow, expecting there to be a lump that makes it difficult to breathe.

But none of those things happen. *Because I'm not losing anything.*

"You guys already kissed me goodbye a long time ago," I say, shrugging. "And I don't know if you intentionally tried to push anyone that might love me away, or if it's a strange coincidence. But you almost had me believing that the best I could do was a man like Tom. *Almost.*"

"I see. *I see.* You have someone in your ear, filling it with garbage. That's what this is, isn't it?"

"You are so wrong." I grin. "It should hurt a lot more than it does to have this conversation. And the fact that it doesn't speaks volumes."

I lean against the cabinet and look at the barn.

Luke was right last night about so much.

"I would never hurt you. Not on purpose. And every decision I made was to save you pain. Do you think boarding the flight home from Cleveland was easy without you? It was one of the worst days of my life. But I did it. I broke my heart because I believed it would save yours."

That's love.

My mother can't even visit me during the holiday season. Heck, I'm lucky to get a call. She hasn't reached out once to see if I'm okay. *What kind of motherly love is that?*

My father thinks it's okay to betray me multiple times over the past seven years by the sound of it. According to him, he made me and built my company, and I'm just an ungrateful little bitch.

That's not love. I've seen what it looks like, and it's not this. And I reject it.

I'm not pretending anymore. I'm not hoping for a miracle. I'm not allowing myself to be hurt so they can win.

It's over. And I'm at peace with that. As much peace as someone can be when realizing just how much your parents don't give a crap about you.

I expect there will be a crash later when the weight of this lands on my heart. But the beauty in it, if there is any, is that Luke will be there to cushion the fall. He'll be there to help me stand back up.

"Dad," I say, my voice calm. "Until you can understand how to be in my life and not poison it, until you can understand what real love looks like, you won't be welcome around me. I'm sorry."

"This isn't over. I'll see you very soon, and we can discuss this face-to-face."

"And I'll have you escorted out. Goodbye, Dad."

I end the call.

My hand shakes as I set the phone down, and my palms are damp. The weight on my shoulders must've been five times heavier than I thought because I'm lightheaded.

And energized.

I need to find someone to spearhead Cotton's concert. I need to prepare my Nashville house for my return early next week. I need to find a new business manager, assistant—because I know her true loyalty lies with my father, and hope to hell I don't need a new boyfriend. Because if that's the case and Luke doesn't want to make this work, I'll be alone forever.

I grab my phone again and find a number. Then I hit *call.*

"Castelli."

"Hey, Troy. It's Laina."

"What can I do for you?"

I smile. "For one, you can stop hiding in the woods like Rambo."

He wants to laugh but restrains himself.

"For two, I know this isn't your job, but I feel like you owe me since you basically stalked me for the past twelve days and got my boyfriend to lie to me."

"I didn't ask him to lie, Ms. Kelley."

"You can play word games all you want, Mr. Castelli, but you made him omit the truth to me, which is lying."

"If you say so."

I laugh. "The next time you're working on my security detail, and I'm in Nashville, I'm going to go on the longest run ever just so you have to follow me."

"That's great, except that you don't run, and I do," he says. "I'm not sure what your point is."

"Damn. You actually like running?"

"Yes, ma'am."

"What do you hate?" I ask.

"Conversations like this, mostly."

"I'm going to hire someone to spy on you and learn all the things you hate to eat and do and hear," I say. "Then I'm going to torture you with all of it as payback."

"Sounds fun. I'm looking forward to it."

"Asshole."

I can hear his smile on the other end of the line.

"Anyway," I say. "I'm getting ready to fire my assistant, so I don't have anyone to call. Can you please arrange for the jet to pick me up tomorrow night and have the Nashville house ready to roll?"

"I suppose."

"Don't trip over yourself to help me out," I say, laughing.

"I'm scrambling. You just can't see me."

"Maybe if I peer through the trees, I can spot you."

"Are we done here?" he asks. "I have calls to make."

I sigh heavily. "Fine. After I get my life sorted, we're sorting yours, Mr. Castelli."

"What makes you think mine's not already sorted?"

"A hunch."

"I'll call you with travel arrangements," he says.

"Or just come on up to the house since you're already here."

"Goodbye, Ms. Kelley."

"Goodbye, Mr. Castelli."

I grin as I hang up.

My phone slides across the table, coming to rest next to the bundle of rope that Luke used on me a few nights ago. My body clenches at the memory.

"We're going to be fine, Luke," I say to the empty room. "I need to make sure you know you belong in my world, and I need to make sure you understand how badly I want to be a part of yours."

I run upstairs. I do my best thinking in the shower.

Chapter Twenty-Four

Luke

"Hey, Megs," I say, walking into Chase's kitchen. "Smells good in here. What's for breakfast?"

"You just missed Chase and Kennedy's bacon and waffles. It was ... a mess, if I'm honest." She laughs. "But Kennedy saw it on Social and wanted to try it. They stuffed the waffles with bacon somehow. I don't know. It was good, just super messy."

"Where is Chase? I need to talk to him."

"Is everything okay?"

My chest tightens. "It will be."

"Okay. Well, he went outside a little while ago. I think he was trying to get out of doing the dishes."

I laugh. "If you see him before I do, tell him I'm outside yelling for him."

"Have a good day, Luke."

"You, too, Megan."

I step outside and look around for my brother. *The bastard probably saw me coming and hid from me.*

I walk to the back of the house and notice the open shed door. Chase comes out of it as I get close.

"Oh, hell," he says, trying not to smile. "You meant it when you said you'd be here this morning. I was hoping you were drinking or something."

"What are you working on?" I ask, nodding to a piece of wood in his hand.

"I'm trying to level a table Megan bought at a flea market last weekend. What about you? What are you working on?"

We walk side by side to a picnic table with a deep, almost purple table on top.

"Looks old," I say.

"Megan says it's an antique, but she thinks everything before the eighties is an antique. I told her the shops slap the word *antique* on shit so people buy it for high prices and feel good about it."

"And this is why I'm here."

Chase gives me a look like our dad does when he doesn't follow along.

I sigh. "I'm here for your asshole logic."

"*What?*"

"This might sound bad," I say, wincing. "But just hear me out and take the point of what I'm saying and not necessarily the words."

"Spit it out, Luke."

"Okay. I need relationship advice, and somehow, you're the resident expert."

He snorts. "How do you figure?"

"You have a wife. You haven't been divorced. And you have a kid. I don't know how that plays into things—in my case, it doesn't—but I feel like that gives you a little extra boost, you know?"

"And I'm smarter than the rest of you," he says.

"And you're an asshole."

He looks up with lifted brows.

"I need an asshole," I say, holding a finger up in the air. "Someone

165

who doesn't get all flowery with their words, overthink it, or care about feelings much. You're perfect."

He rolls his eyes.

"I've been seeing an old girlfriend for a couple of weeks," I say, keeping things as vague as possible. "And I don't know how to make her understand that, unlike her dad and ex, I'm not here to hurt her. I don't get off on putting her in her place or hurting her feelings."

"They did that?"

"Yes, they did."

"Beat the fuck out of them."

I laugh, nodding appreciatively. "Okay. Not the question I needed answered, but I like your moxie today."

"You should've seen these damn waffles Kennedy wanted this morning. We had batter and bacon grease everywhere." He mocks the wood up to the chair. "I came out here because I didn't want to clean it up."

"Dick move."

He stares at me for a moment before going back to his project. "My wife will be properly repaid for her assistance. I promise you that."

"This isn't about you. This is about me. Can we focus here? I'm on a deadline."

"Please proceed."

"How do I get her to understand that she can trust me?"

"Be trustable."

"Not helpful, Chase."

He looks at me through the chair legs. "I mean it. Every time something comes up that you can use to build her trust, do it. Everyone is trustworthy until it's time to do trustworthy shit."

"That's it?"

He sighs. "Look, Luke. I'm not a relationship kind of guy. I might be married, but that's because Megan is literally the only person in the world that I could be with."

166

"That's how I feel about ... my girl." *Don't slip up. Don't say her name.*

"I don't have to really work on my relationship with Megan. We have date nights, and I get her flowers on Fridays when I grab pizza on my way home for movie night. But the rest of it is just day-to-day stuff. Showing up. Being the guy I say I am—the man I want to be. Shit like that. If you want her to trust you, show up as the trustworthy guy. Do it consistently, and she won't have a reason not to believe you."

"Okay, okay. You're pretty good at this."

He shrugs, turning his attention back to the chair.

"I have one more thing," I say.

"Hurry up. You're starting to get on my nerves."

"Rude." I sit on the bench. "What would you do if, say, Megan had a super famous job? And she couldn't leave it, and you didn't want her to. But you also really liked your life and what you do here. How do you make that work?"

Chase stands, narrowing his eyes. He lifts a brow.

I smile.

He nods and goes back to the task at hand. "If Megs was a musician, let's say, and I ran a business out of the shed, I'd decide what's most important and adjust."

"But what if you were ... a welder," I say. "And Dad welded, and so did Grandpa. And you're the new generation of welders in the family. Could you walk away from that?"

Chase sets the block down and plants his hands on the picnic table. He watches me, amused.

"If Megan wanted to go to the moon, I'd buy the three of us tickets, and off we'd go," he says. "Because there's nothing more important to me than my wife. *Not a damn fucking thing.*"

He's right. I knew it before I came here. But I just needed to hear it from him to be sure.

"Are we done now?" my brother asks. "You're either going to help or hit the road."

"I'm out of here. Thanks, Chase."

"Bye."

I walk across the lawn to my truck, formulating a plan.

"We got this, Laina. You need to realize that I'll do anything for you."

And I mean anything.

Chapter Twenty-Five

Laina

I fold the last towel and place it back in the bin.

Since the call with my father, I've been full of nervous energy. I'm too twitchy to sit still. I can't quiet my mind. Something is off with Dad. He was too bold, even for him.

Between worrying about him and anxiously waiting for Luke to return, I'm all over the place. The only thing that helped me calm down was folding laundry. I folded the load in the dryer from three days ago, everything in my suitcase—which needed it anyway—and Luke's T-shirts. They were in desperate need of help.

I've practiced my speech countless times, ensuring that I cover my bases. There must be an apology, an admission of wrongdoing, and a plan of attack to improve. To do better. At least, that's what the publicist on Social suggested. It sounded better than anything I free balled—most of which ended up in a ramble and tears.

I can do better than that.

The only hiccup I foresee between Luke and me would be if he chose not to engage with my music life. He may think it's too nasty and too complicated. He may see what it's done to me and not want anything to do with it. He may very well think it will be the source of constant conflict and a massive headache—and he wouldn't be wrong.

And I can't blame him for worrying about that.

But I have hope, *a lot of it*, that he'll love me more than he hates my job.

The roar of an engine breaks the silence, and I hold my breath, waiting for Luke's truck to fly around the corner of the house and park in front of the barn. But that doesn't happen. Instead, the vehicle seems to stop in front of the house, and multiple doors open and close.

Who the hell is that?

I abandon the laundry basket and head for the entryway. The doorbell rings as I reach for the handle. *Good timing.* My heart pounds as I pull it toward me ... and nearly collapse onto the floor.

My father and Tom stand on Luke's porch. A short, redheaded man with a phone aimed directly at my face is between them, tucked behind their elbows as if he predicts an explosion.

What the fuck?

Nausea clings to my stomach muscles, and sweat slides down my back. Dad's words that I took as a warning were really a threat. *"This isn't over. We'll see each other very soon, and we can discuss this face-to-face."*

I'm going to be sick.

Dad slips his sunglasses down his nose. The glimmer in his eye is distressing. "See, Tom? I told you we'd find her."

God, please help me.

My stomach lurches like I might actually vomit all over them.

Troy's SUV bolts up the driveway, rocks and dust flying behind it. I've never been happier to see him. Because while I don't want to think this isn't going to go super sideways and get physical, *who knows anymore?* I didn't dream either would show up at Luke's, let alone together.

Nothing is off the table.

Dad reeks of desperation and oozes fury. Tom is just happy to watch me suffer—hence the camera. I'm sure that was his idea. He's planning on watching this on repeat. He loves nothing more than seeing himself as the show's star ... especially when he gets to dominate others in the process.

Tom stands tall, all six feet, four inches towering over me in a sad display of superiority.

I almost feel sorry for him.

Troy slides his car next to the garage and is out the door before it fully stops. He marches across the driveway in his suit. He's pissed.

"Troy," I cry, so thankful that he hadn't actually left me.

"Easy now, *Troy,*" Dad says, turning his charm on my security guard. The condescension in his voice is utterly embarrassing. *Has he always spoken to my team like this?* "How have you been, son? I haven't seen you for a while."

"I'm not *your son.* This is private property. You need to go. *Now.*"

Tom makes a face like he's looking at a puppy nipping at his pant leg. "Why don't you get back in your car?" His features morph into steel, and the real Tom comes out. "This doesn't concern you."

Troy doesn't flinch. He might even look amused.

"Stop filming me," I say, perturbed by the camera trained on my features.

"Listen, doll," Tom says, patronizing me. "You obviously need therapy after this ugly little tantrum you've thrown over the past two weeks. And I have access to the best therapists in the world. I'm willing to look past your attention-wanting behavior and pay out the nose to repair our reputations." He leans forward, a sick snicker on his face. "I'll still marry you if you promise to get the help you *so desperately* need."

"What I *desperately need* is for you two pricks to get out of here and forget I exist," I say, looking him dead in the eye.

"I'm only going to say this once," Troy says, his voice cutting through the tension like a knife. "Get off the porch, or I'll move you. One option is much easier and cleaner, but it's really up to you."

171

Tom rolls his eyes and looks at Troy like he's bored. "*Or what?* You're not going to do jack shit. Now stand over there and shut the fuck up."

Troy steps toward him with a look on his face that I've only seen once before. It ended with a lot of blood—not Troy's. And while it would give me a thrill to see Tom put in his place, especially since he dared to come to Luke's and talk to me this way, I also know the PR machine behind my ex, and I don't want that spinning against me even more.

"Troy, don't," I say just as another vehicle comes down the driveway.

It's Luke's truck, and it's picking up speed. *Oh no.*

My heart races, and I grab the door for support. I have no idea what's about to happen, and the thought of how many ways this could go wrong terrifies me.

"Ah, is that the Marshall boy?" Dad asks, his head turning back to me slowly. "I see."

"Who is the Marshall boy?" Tom asks.

"A little punk that Laina used to date until I got rid of him. I did you a favor, little girl."

No, you didn't. I step onto the porch, squaring my shoulders to my father.

"That *little punk* is the best man I know," I say. "He's kind and good and honest. He treats people well and me even better. The two of you could take notes if you didn't have your heads so far up your fucking asses."

Tom sighs. "Two weeks and you have such a filthy mouth."

"You should hear the things I say to Luke," I say, smirking.

The fury on Tom's face is worth every problem my *filthy mouth* will cause me.

Dad wraps his hand around my arm, making me yelp.

Troy suddenly grabs my father by the back of his shirt with such force that my father loses his footing. He stumbles down the stairs backward, swiping wildly for the railing. The only reason he doesn't fall on his ass is because Troy has a hold of him.

"Touch her again, and you'll die," Troy says, his face inches from Dad's.

Luke jumps out of his truck, his eyes wild with confusion and fury. He runs across the driveway, making a beeline for me.

Tom's laugh is loud and obnoxious. His eyes are filled with humor.

"You left me for *that?*" he asks. "Oh, Laina. Don't do this to yourself."

"What the hell is going on here?" Luke asks, storming up the steps and placing himself between me and Tom. His body ripples with unbridled fury beneath his purple feed store shirt.

I place a hand on Luke's shoulder, tears filling my eyes.

Troy releases Dad, shoving him away from the steps.

Tom makes a show out of looking Luke up and down. "Wow. Interesting choice, Laina. It seems when you go low, you go to the bottom of the barrel."

"Get the fuck out of here," Luke says, not at all intimidated by Tom's overconfidence.

Tom ignores him. "Isn't it humiliating to be caught at your boyfriend's house when you were supposed to be on your honeymoon with me right now?" He shakes his head. "Don't you have any shame?"

"Oh, I'm ashamed of a lot of things, Tom. But none of it has to do with Luke."

"Luke, huh?" Tom smirks at him. "Nice to meet ya, *Luke.*"

"Is this the life you want?" Dad says, straightening his shirt. "Why would you choose this? Tom can give you the best of every-thing—access to anyone, anywhere you can dream. What's this guy gonna give you? Fleas?"

Luke bristles beneath my touch.

"You realize that I don't need Tom, or you, or anyone for that matter, to give me anything money can buy, right?" I ask, grinning at him. "Because Dad—I have a lot of it. Granted, you have a lot of it because you stole it from me."

"Tread lightly, little girl," he says, narrowing his eyes.

"Or what? What are you possibly going to do to me? Record this and sell it to the tabloids to try to further whatever fucked-up agenda you have?" I laugh. "Fine. Do it. I don't care."

Troy places his hand over the top of the phone, making the redhead jump. He squeezes the phone so hard that something inside it crunches. The redhead's eyes widen, and he steps back, leaving the phone in Troy's hand.

"It looks like we took care of that," I say, stepping beside Luke. He takes my hand and squeezes it, and the warmth of the contact spreads through my veins. "The only thing I need from anyone is love, Dad. And you and Tom are incapable of that."

"We're capable of what's important. We have our priorities straight, Laina," Tom says. "Life isn't about a stupid emotion meant to make businesses money and provide a source of entertainment for simple-minded fools. Don't be a sheep."

"My God. Will you listen to yourselves?" I ask. "Go. I never want to see either of you ever again."

"You're coming with us," Dad says. "We aren't leaving you here when it's clear you need a mental evaluation."

I look at Luke. He watches me for a sign that I need his help. The fact that he realizes I need to do this on my own and that all I need is for him to be here beside me means the world.

"How can you want to be with this guy?" Tom asks, jamming a finger Luke's way. "He just stands there like a bitch."

Luke chuckles angrily, licking his bottom lip. "She's doing just fine on her own. That's the thing that neither of you understand. *She doesn't need to be saved.* Laina is strong and smart, and she can make her own decisions. She can certainly handle the two of you. If she needs me, I'm right here, ready to kill a motherfucker."

"Oh, is that how it is?" Tom asks, standing taller.

Luke grins. "That's how it is."

"Okay then," Tom says, switching his gaze to me. "Enjoy your life being a little whore—*fuck!*"

He barely gets the word out when Luke grabs him by the front of his shirt and headbutts him in the nose. Blood runs down Tom's face, mixing with the tears that come automatically.

Shit. My hands fly to my mouth as Tom tries to regain his composure. Luke stares at him like a predator about to strike its prey.

"You asshole!" Tom shouts, backing down the stairs.

Luke matches him step for step. His back is flexed, his shoulders taut.

The redhead runs to their truck and jumps inside.

"You can't do that," Dad shouts, clawing at any shred of control he can find.

"He just fucking did." Troy again grabs Dad by the back of his shirt and drags him to the truck. "It would be best if I didn't see you again. Do you understand?"

Tom stands at the side of the truck, trying frantically to get the bleeding to stop.

"I really hope we've made ourselves clear," Luke says, walking up to him. "But if you ever need a refresher course, let me know."

"Fuck you," Tom says, giving up and letting the blood flow down his face. "Fuck you both."

He grabs his door handle and yanks it open.

"One last thing," Troy says, grinning. "I have this all on camera from my car. If you want to pull any shit, take it up with Landry Security's attorneys."

Tom gives me one final glare before getting into the truck. My dad starts it up, revving the engine in some childish display of aggression, and then rips it down Luke's driveway.

I exhale, my shoulders falling forward. Luke is at my side in a second. His arms go around me, holding me tight.

"Are you okay?" he asks.

"I am now."

He squeezes me, pressing a kiss to the top of my head.

"If anyone asks, I headbutted Tom," Troy says, heading back to his car.

Luke releases me. "What do you mean?"

"Weren't you recording it?" I ask, confused. "Wouldn't they see that it was Luke?"

Troy opens his door and leans against it. "Seems like my camera wasn't on." He winks at us and then takes his seat. "I'll sit up here for a while. Let me know if you need anything."

"Thank you, Troy," I say.

He pauses, leaning his head out of the car. "Do me a favor, Laina."

"Anything."

"Stop being so damn stubborn. The next time the people who love you decide you need protection, fucking just take it."

I laugh as Luke nudges me from the side.

"Lesson learned," I say.

Troy mutters something before shutting the door.

Luke spins me around to face him, holding my face in his hands. "We have a lot to talk about."

"Wanna go inside?"

He chuckles.

"What?" I ask.

"We're off to a good start."

"Why is that?"

He kisses me gently. "Because you just asked me if I wanted to go inside my house like you're the one who lives here."

Hope blossoms in my chest, and I'm not scared to grab ahold of it.

"Because I do," I say, tugging his hand. "Let's go talk."

He gives me his sweetest, most crooked smile and follows me into our house.

Chapter Twenty-Six

Laina

"What the hell happened?" Luke asks, pouring us a glass of tea. I think it's out of habit more than anything. "I was just gone for a couple of hours."

I collapse in a chair at the table. I can feel the adrenaline ease, and the aftereffects make me shiver.

"I was just folding laundry and preparing my speech to give you when you got home," I say. "And I heard a truck and thought it was you. Obviously, it wasn't."

He hands me a glass and then scoots his chair closer to me. As expected, he sets his tea on the table and doesn't even take a drink.

"What kind of speech were you preparing?" he asks.

"I don't know. It was kind of like the State of the Union but with fewer politics and more promise of sex."

"You know, that's a good analogy. Because whether you were going to fuck me over or promise me illicit things to get what you want, it works."

I laugh.

He lays a hand on my thigh as if he can't bear not touching me.

"I never want to do last night again," I say, touching the side of his handsome face.

"Me either. I resorted to texting my siblings in the middle of the night just for a distraction. It was that bad."

"You could've come to bed with me."

"I know. But I thought you needed some space. I probably did, too."

"This is so hard for me because it's like looking in the mirror and seeing a huge zit on your forehead the day you have a date with your crush."

"I better be the crush in this scenario."

I giggle. *And this is why I love you, Luke Marshall.*

"You're the crush in every scenario," I say.

He presses a sweet kiss to my lips. I want to lean into him and have him hold me, to forget the past eighteen hours and get back to being us. But last night proved that we have some things to clear up if we're going to go forward.

And we must go forward. He's the other half of my heart.

"I'm not making excuses for myself," I say, "but I truly never realized until last night how scared I am. Admitting that makes me squirm because it's being so vulnerable, so exposed. It's like I'm opening myself up all the way to my soul. I walk around with a shield half-cocked all the time."

"Of course, you do. You don't have to explain that. I don't know anyone in the world who could navigate your life without being on edge at least a little."

I smile at him. "I want you to know that I love you, Luke, with all my heart. And I know you love me, too. I can see it in how you look at me, touch me, and are willing to sacrifice for me. Even though you didn't see me in Cleveland, it was a selfless act. I see that now. I think I was so upset and angry—mostly at my father—that it got all muddy, and I just drowned in the depths of it all."

"I would do anything for you. I mean that."

Tears pool in my eyes. "It's the little things for me—the shirts from the feed store, your kindness when you realized I basically broke into your house because I didn't know where to go, and you making me work in the barn because you somehow knew that I needed a shot of normalcy. That's love, Luke. And I would have to be blind and deaf and unable to feel your touch not to know you love me."

"Sounds like you do get me, after all."

"We'll have rough patches. All relationships do. And I want those for us so we can work through them, grow a scar over the wound, and have that part of us be impenetrable."

"Don't say penetrate."

I grin.

He squeezes my thigh and then sits back in his chair. "I'm sorry that I didn't tell you about Cleveland and that I kept Troy's presence from you."

"Well, obviously I'm glad you did that now."

We laugh softly.

"I won't keep anything from you again," he says.

"And I won't assume every little thing is a conspiracy either. I need to relax a little."

"Taking control of your life will help. You're building a new team, right? Get people you can trust and who are loyal to you. Surround yourself with people who make your soul feel good."

I take a sip of tea and sigh. *Now comes the tricky part.*

I get up from the table and move aimlessly through the room. My brain works better when I'm on my feet, and I need my brain to work overtime now.

How do I bring up the fact that I have to leave soon? What if he wants me to split my time at work and at home? Because I can't always do that. And I can't ask him to give up his work either. It's such a big part of him.

"What are you thinking?" he asks.

Just go for it. "If we're doing this—"

"Oh, we're doing this."

I grin. "Then how does it work? I've already decided that I'm going to pull back on a lot of things. I didn't want to be this busy to begin with, but my former business manager had a habit of using me like a show pony."

Luke's jaw sets.

"But even if I do that, I will be gone a lot. And when I'm here regularly, I'll always have to have security around—even when I'm not. Because people are absolutely delusional. You have no idea."

He finally takes a drink of his precious tea.

"I feel like I'm so much to deal with, that my life is so big in so many ways that wanting to be with me means having to accept all of this, too," I say, my words falling faster. "And that feels unfair to even ask of you, Luke. If I'm in your life, it will turn it upside down. It'll change in ways I can't even predict."

My heart thunders as I wait for his response. I don't know if he's thought about all of that. I assume he has to some extent. But I need to make sure he knows what he's getting into before he chooses me.

He lowers his glass, uncovering a smirk. "Are you done?"

"What?"

He sighs. "I'm not walking away from you again, Laina. Even if you take me to the edges of the earth and demand we stay there, I'll pack your favorite snacks."

"Oh, Luke ..."

"We can't have all the answers right now because, like you said, we can't predict everything that will come at us. But that's the thing—it'll be coming *at us*. Not you. Not me. *Us*."

I blink back tears.

"My world has never felt righter than it has these past two weeks," he says. "And it's not just having you around that's made it so amazing. It's being able to make you smile. To hear your laughter. To do little things that make your eyes light up."

"Why are you so good to me?"

He grins. "Because you're my girl. My life began the day I met you, and the only way it makes sense is when we're together."

"But what about me having to be gone so much? I have to leave Monday."

"Then you go and work and have a ball. Enjoy the fruits of your labor. If you need me, I'm a phone call away."

My throat is sticky with emotion. "And what about all the changes around here?"

"As long as they come with a new closet for your shit, I'll manage."

I laugh. It grows louder as relief and joy spread through me.

"Anything else you want to cover?" he asks.

I stare at the barn and consider what our future will look like. I still want to make music. It's a huge part of who I am. But I also want to spend afternoons in the barn, mornings folding clothes, and late nights eating pizza in bed and listening to Luke's stories. I want to watch my man work and learn more about his business. I want to be a champion of his life like he is mine.

It can happen.

I don't know much, but I know this much is true—love is real. It's good. Love doesn't hurt you or try to shrink you. It waters your seeds and shines light so you can grow. It's everything I read about in books. I didn't think that was possible. But I know, thanks to the love of a sexy, green-eyed, tattooed farrier who has the key to my heart.

"That was the best damn State of the Union speech I've ever heard," Luke says, grinning. "But can we get to the promises of illicit activities part of it? I really want to use that rope again."

My stomach flutters. "How about this ..."

He reaches for me and brings my mouth to his. The kiss is just like Luke. It's strong, yet soft. Sweet, yet ... not. It holds promises for the future while not missing a beat now.

Luke Marshall proves one thing—true love never ends.

Now that I've found it again, I'm never letting it, *never letting Luke*, go.

Epilogue

L aina

Six months later ...

"Hey, Laina! Do you still have my pink boots?" Kennedy calls from Maggie's mudroom.

"Yikes. I think so. Do you need them?" I ask.

She pokes her head around the corner and grins. "Not until this weekend. Dad finally agreed to let me go to a party, but only because Megan intervened on my behalf. But it's behind one of my friend's houses. It's supposed to rain the day before, so I thought boots might be smart."

"Yours smell like horse shit." I wince. "How about this. I'll buy you a pair and have them shipped to your house by Friday?"

"Yes!" she says. "I freaking love you, Laina."

Gavin waits until Kennedy's gone before lifting a brow. His arms cross over his chest.

"What?" I ask innocently. "Why do you look so mad?"

"You're playing dirty."

"Excuse me?"

"You can't try to get to the top of the favorites list by buying her shit."

I shrug. "I don't know. It seems to be working."

He narrows his eyes. "When do you leave again?"

"Two weeks. I have a mini tour in Europe. Why?"

"Because I have to figure out how to sabotage you while you're gone."

"*Gavin!*" I say, laughing. "Don't threaten me. I could always fly her to London."

Chase walks in, shaking his head. "You aren't flying my daughter to London just to get higher on the favorites list."

"Chase, you are no fun," I say.

Gavin walks by him and winks.

I gasp. "You can't do that! You can't work covertly with Chase to shut me down."

Gavin shrugs. "I don't know. It seems to be working."

The door opens, and the noise level goes up a hundred points. Megan and Kate, both women whom I've grown to absolutely adore, come in laughing. Maggie and Kennedy, who must've gone out the back door and then around the house, follow. Lonnie trails them by a few steps, yelling at Gavin to get the rest of the groceries from the car. Luke brings up the end with his arms full of bags.

It's beautiful chaos.

"What can I do, Maggie?" I ask, meeting everyone in the kitchen.

"Oh, sweetheart. You made it." Her face lights up as she pulls me in for a hug. "Luke said your flight was delayed due to bad weather."

"We were stuck on the tarmac for a while, but it was fine once we got in the air."

Luke slides in for a quick kiss even though he picked me up from the airport and hasn't really stopped kissing me since.

The past six months have been a little bumpy. Overhauling my management team while starting a relationship with a man who lives hours away from the office has resulted in many long nights, plane rides, and shifting schedules. But now that the team is set with Hollis Hudson at the helm—a professional relationship flourishing beautifully—everything has started to smooth out.

It's taken restraining orders and cease and desist letters for Tom and my father to finally leave me alone, but the past month has been peaceful. Hollis discovered that my father was getting kickbacks on many of my deals and was investing a lot of that money into various business arrangements with Tom.

Sucks for them.

On the other hand, Luke has adapted well to fortifying his home with security cameras. He didn't even object to the fence Landry Security insisted be placed around the property and a guard house at the base of the driveway. He rolls his eyes about it a lot, but I think he secretly thinks it's amusing.

"Did you ever make that lasagna, Laina?" Maggie asks, busying herself with putting groceries away.

Kate gives me a look and tries not to laugh.

Maggie and this damn lasagna.

"Yeah," I say, without telling her I made it so that I could say I did when she inevitably asked. "It was good. Luke loved it."

"Luke will eat anything," Lonnie says.

My cheeks flush. *If they only knew ...*

"Are you going to be in Nashville next week?" I ask Kate. "Did that meeting get set up?"

"Oh, yes! I am. I get there on Wednesday. When do you go back?"

"Tuesday. Why don't you stay with me? I have a great view and lots of wine. And you can get your sweater back that I borrowed last month."

"Sold!" she says, laughing.

Kennedy sits at a barstool and plucks a cookie off the peanut butter board that Megan is putting together.

"Dammit," Luke says from the dining room. "Where the hell did I put it?"

"Put what?" I ask.

"I had a box in my pocket, and it's gone." He frowns. "It could be anywhere."

"Do you need help?" I ask.

"I can't see under the table. It's too dark."

"Here. Use my phone as a flashlight."

I go into the dining area and hand him my phone. But instead of taking it, he takes my hand instead.

The whole family stands silently around the kitchen with big smiles. Megan gives me a sneaky thumbs-up.

Oh. My. God.

Luke takes the phone from my hand and sets it on the table. Then he gets down on one knee.

There's no buildup. *I just cry.*

He gazes up at me with a sincerity that hits my heart so hard that I can't breathe.

"First, I want to point out that I realize we have a crowd, and I know you explicitly hated the last proposal you got in front of a crowd," he says. "But my mother would've killed me had she not gotten to witness this since Chase proposed in a mud puddle outside of The Wet Whistle."

Everyone laughs, including me, through my tears.

"I love you," he says. "I could try to add on a bunch of random phrases like more than the moon and stars or more than the universe. But none even begin to capture how I feel about you."

"Oh, Luke. That's so sweet," Maggie says before getting shushed by our family.

"You don't have to marry me soon," he says, rubbing his thumb over the top of my hand. "And you don't have to marry me in public. We don't even have to get married if you don't want to."

"Doesn't that defeat the point of asking her to marry you?" Gavin asks.

I sigh and look at my brother. "You're missing the point. I want her to know I'm not pressuring her to do anything. I'm just stating my intention that I plan to be with her forever. And she can do what she wants with that information."

"Stop talking to Gavin. Talk to me," I say, laughing.

He clears his throat. "Right. Sorry." He takes a small wooden box out of his pocket and opens it. The most beautiful, simplest, most perfect ring I've ever seen sits proudly in the center. "Laina Kelley, will you marry me?"

"I love you," I whisper, getting a shy grin in return.

"Is that a *yes*?"

I laugh, shaking my finger at him. He slides the ring on just before I launch myself in his arms.

"*Yes*," I say, kissing him. "Yes. I will marry you."

Our family cheers, and Maggie pulls out bottles of champagne that she had run to the grocery store to pick up, unbeknownst to me. *And I thought she was getting stuff to make lasagna.*

Luke holds me tight in his arms and kisses the shell of my ear. "Mom is making dinner. Eat fast. I want to get you home."

Home.

I want to get you home.

Doesn't he know that home is right here, in his arms?

I take my fiancé's face in my hands and kiss him again.

"Did you make this ring?" I ask, inspecting the craftsmanship.

"Yeah. I looked at some stores, but they all looked the same. I couldn't sleep one night without you and got the idea to make you one myself with my blacksmith tools." He bites his lip. "If you don't like it, we'll get you something else."

I smile, shaking my head. "If I could have my choice, this is what I would've chosen."

"Really?"

"Really." I kiss the shell of his ear. "It will take your mom at least an hour to make dinner. If we act fast, we could sneak home for a quickie and be back before it's time to eat."

I giggle as he stands and pulls me behind him.

Guess he liked that idea.

I guarantee he'll love what's to come.

He doesn't know I have a surprise of my own. It'll just take another eight months to arrive.

Author's Note: If you haven't read Chase's book, MORE THAN I COULD, it's live now on Amazon and Audible.

More from Adriana

The Proposal—Chapter One
   Blakely

"Could you die quietly?" Ella sighs, pulling her sunglasses down and squinting into the sunlight. "And maybe do it over there, please?"

Two quintessential frat boys, a label I'd bet my life on yet feels like a disservice to fraternities everywhere, cease their constant complaints about being hungover. Their whining is a show, a pathetic effort to gain attention, and one we're over—especially Ella.

They fire a dirty look at my best friend. She cocks a brow, challenging them right back, and waits.

Lying on the chaise next to her, I smirk. *How many seconds will it take for them to realize they're outgunned by a five-foot-three pistol with bubble-gum pink toenails?*

Eight ... Nine ... Ten ...

They gather their things quietly, watching Ella like she might toss them into the pool if they don't act quickly enough.

I wouldn't be shocked if that happened, either.

Ella St. James doesn't surprise me much anymore. She carried a tray of freshly baked snickerdoodle cookies when she rang my doorbell three years ago. She was adorable, wearing an apron with embroidered cherries and a white silk ribbon in her hair while welcoming me to the Nashville neighborhood. It starkly contrasted with the following weekend when she took me out so I could *get acquainted with the city.* That night ended with Ella jacking some guy's jaw for trying to grope me on the dance floor and me picking her up from the police station in an Uber at three in the morning.

"Thank you," she says, sliding the glasses up her nose and returning to her book.

Las Vegas is sweltering. Blue water sparkles just inches from our feet, and I swear it only amplifies the sun's rays. We should probably get a massage or go shopping to beat the unbearable heat, but I didn't fly for almost four hours to stay inside.

I could've celebrated my new job and birthday like that in Tennessee.

"How do you think I would look with red hair?" I ask, stretching my legs in front of me. "Not bright cherry red, but a more purple-y, crimson-y red."

"No."

I furrow my brows. "That wasn't a yes or no question."

"I was cutting to the chase." Her fingertip trails along the bottom of the paperback. "That's not the question you were really asking."

It wasn't? I settle against my chair. *Yeah, it wasn't.*

It was a last-minute attempt at being young and reckless before I turn thirty tomorrow.

This whole birthday crap has been a bit of a mind fuck.

I've lived the past ten years with little abandon. I've traveled, dated, and swam with sharks. Went on a ten-city tour with a rock band. Attended a movie premiere, got engaged (and unengaged), and ate pizza at the world's oldest pizzeria in Naples. *Check that off the bucket list.* And with every year of fun, I assumed I had nothing to worry about—that I would have my shit together before I turned thirty and became a real adult.

That was an incorrect assumption.

By all accounts, I should be in a stable relationship and burdened with a mortgage and enough debt to bury my soul until Jesus returns. Appliances should excite me. I should have a baby. *I should understand life insurance.* Instead, I just broke up with *another* bad boy with commitment issues, re-upped the rental contract on my townhouse, and refilled my birth control.

But that all ends in six hours. I have to turn over a new leaf when the sun comes up. It's time.

Ella's book snaps closed. "This is not a tri-life crisis, Blakely. It's just a birthday."

"I know that."

"But do you?"

"*Yes, I do,*" I say, mocking her. "I'm not in crisis mode. I'm just transitioning into this new era of buying eye cream and freezing my eggs, and it's a little ... terrifying."

She sighs. "You've been buying eye cream for years."

"Yeah, as a hedge against the future. This *is* the future."

Ella rolls onto her side, brushing her dark hair off her shoulder. "While I can't relate because I have a solid two years before I'm thirty—"

"Was that necessary?"

She laughs. "You're freaking out for no reason. Tomorrow is just another day."

"I know. *I really do.* There's just this pressure to get my ducks in a row and start making serious progress, or else I'll be fifty with no husband or kids. And I want both."

"All I ask is that you be a little more selective on the husband part because the last few guys you've dated ..." She whistles. "Not good, Blakely."

Yeah, I know.

"I know you feel your biological clock ticking or whatever it is, but you *have* been doing big things," she says. "You're the new artist manager assistant at Mason Music Label. Remember, you little badass? That's impressive."

I shrug happily at the reminder. That's true—a dream come true, really. *And even more of a reason to get my shit together.* "But would I be even more impressive as a redhead?"

"The answer is still no."

I groan. "*Come on.* I want to go out on something big. Something fun. Something wild that I'll remember while I'm taking vitamins and going to bed before ten."

Ella reaches for her water. "Fine. But let's find something else. Red doesn't suit your skin tone."

"Like what? I'm not getting anything pierced, and I don't think I'm ready to commit to a tattoo."

"You've been wanting a tattoo since the day I met you. As a matter of fact, weren't you looking at tattoos when I brought over those cookies?"

I laugh. "Yes. But it's so permanent. What if I don't want it next week?"

She rolls her eyes.

"What else is there?" I ask. "Let's think."

"Well, you could find a man with money and get a quickie wedding on the Strip."

I laugh again, turning over onto my stomach. "At this point, that's the only way I'll get married—inebriated and to a stranger." *The guys I date aren't marriage material. I'll probably be alone forever at this rate.*

"Hey, people find love in all sorts of ways."

"True, but the odds that I'll find a marry-able man in the next few hours is incredibly low." I fold my arms under my head. "In lieu of sexy strangers with an engagement ring in their pocket, what else do you suggest?"

She taps a finger to her lips. "We could go to a show tonight. A male striptease or something like that. It might be a way to get your juices flowing—"

"*Ew!*"

"*While lacking permanence.* Then just see where the night takes us. Be free-spirited."

"You just want to go because it's one more way to needle Brock."

Her grin is full of mischief. "So? What's your point?"

Ella and my brother have been *a thing* for almost two years. *What kind of thing?* I'm afraid to label it, although I'm fairly certain they're exclusive without declaring exclusivity.

On the one hand, Ella is a lot to handle. She's smart, opinionated, and doesn't need a man—and she knows it. She also has a propensity to make decisions and weigh the risks after. That drives Brock nuts.

On the other hand, dating Brock would be a nightmare. Women throw themselves at him wherever he goes. Men stop him for autographs and to *man-swoon* over him. And during the season, he's focused and mostly unavailable. That doesn't always work for Ella.

I watch this back-and-forth and vow never to get into a relationship with a player—an athlete or otherwise. *Again.* I've done that before, and it didn't end well.

"I'm taking it you two are still fighting," I say.

"We aren't fighting. There's nothing to fight about." She lifts her chin to the sky. "I'm right, and he's wrong. That's all there is to it."

"I agree. You're right this time."

Her eyes widen. "*You're damn right I'm right.* I'm not putting up with him taking off to Miami with his friends and not even mentioning our anniversary."

"How can you have an anniversary if you aren't in an official relationship?" I snicker. "Isn't that what you always tell me? That you aren't in an official relationship with him?"

She waves a hand through the air, dismissing my question. "It's a prelationship, but that doesn't change anything in this circumstance."

"A *what?*"

"A *prelationship.* The formative stage where boundaries and expectations are established so you can determine if the other person is willing to abide by them." She pauses. "*Brock isn't.*"

I roll my eyes and let it go. They'll settle this before Brock returns from Miami and we're home from Vegas. I've seen it too many times to count.

"Then fine," I say, sitting up. "Let's go to a show. But if my brother asks whose idea it was, I'm not taking the blame."

"Tell him it was mine. *I want him to know.* A little competition never hurt anyone."

"Competition for your non-boyfriend?" I ask, grinning.

"Precisely."

I shake my head as a bead of sweat trickles down my face. I wipe it away with the back of my hand. "I'm ready to go in and grab a shower."

"And I need to make reservations for dinner." She sits up, slipping on her flip-flops. "You owe me, you know."

"What do I owe you for?"

"For depriving me of my right as your best friend to throw you the most outrageous, amazing birthday party that Nashville has ever seen." She stuffs her water bottle in her bag. "I'm known in certain circles as the girl who throws the best bashes. I can only wonder what everyone is thinking about this."

I laugh at her ridiculousness, slipping my cover-up over my head. "You've thrown me a huge birthday party every year I've known you. You can miss this one. It won't hurt."

She frowns. "Maybe it won't hurt *you*, but it pains *me*. I have a reputation to uphold."

"You'll survive."

I drop my phone, towel, and water bottle into my bag. I skim the area around me to ensure I have everything.

"Ready?" she asks.

"Yeah." A bubble of excitement fills me. *Let the birthday festivities commence.* "Let's go find trouble."

Ella shares my smile as we slide our bags on our sun-kissed shoulders. I spot my book under her chair and grab it. *How did it get there?*

As I stand, my gaze falls on Ella. Her wide eyes are twinkling. I've seen this look enough times to know things are about to get real.

"What?" I ask, frozen in place.

Her grin pulls wider. "I think trouble just found us."

Oh no.

Find out what happens here.

Available now on Amazon and Audible.

Acknowledgments

Thank you to my Creator for all the blessings in my life.

This job would be impossible without the love and support of my husband, Saul, and our boys. Like Luke says, I could use many clique terms, but none would come close to how much I love you.

My bonus parents are so patient and understanding when they come to visit, and I'm holed up in my office on a deadline. I love you, Peggy and Rob.

Thank you to Kari March for designing the perfect cover and to Wander Aguiar and his team for helping me secure the only photo that would've worked for this book.

I want to shout out fellow authors, Kaylee Ryan, for helping me when I was stuck in blurb hell and Jessica Prince for writing with me every single day. (I'm back, I'm back—ha!) Sending love to Dylan Allen for joining us for writing springs. I believe in you!

Of course, I send my love to my best friend Mandi Beck for keeping an eye on things while I'm away. And S.L. Scott is the best cheerleader and encourager a girl could ever want. Love you. Also, a shoutout to Anjelica Grace, the real one, not the fake one, for hanging with me while I carved out this story. Kenna Rey is my first set of eyes and ears on most of my books and I couldn't do it without her. Thanks, too, to Michele Ficht for her endless enthusiasm and optimism.

When working with me, my editors go through a lot—that's putting it lightly. Big hugs to Marion Archer for being by my side the whole way through and doing whatever it takes to get the job done.

You are the best. And a high-five to Jenny Sims for always opening a spot for me. For once, we weren't down to the very last minute. Let's write that down.

As always, a huge thank you to the women who help me and my groups run smoothly—Tiffany Remy, Kaitie Reister, Stephanie Gibson, Jordan Fazzini, and Sue Maturo. You're the best!

The team at Valentine PR is amazing. Thank you, everyone, for your patience and hard work. Especially you, Kim Cermak. God bless you. LOL

Last but certainly not least, thank you to my readers. I get to tell stories for a living because of you. I'm forever grateful.

About the Author

USA Today Bestselling author, Adriana Locke, writes contemporary romances about the two things she knows best—big families and small towns. Her stories are about ordinary people finding extraordinary love with the perfect combination of heart, heat, and humor.

She loves connecting with readers, fall weather, football, reading alpha heroes, everything pumpkin, and pretending to garden.

Hailing from a tiny town in the Midwest, Adriana spends her free time with her high school sweetheart (who she married over twenty years ago) and their four sons (who truly are her best work).

Her kitchen may be a perpetual disaster, and if all else fails, there is always pizza.

Join her reader group and talk all the bookish things by clicking here.

www.adrianalocke.com

$15.00

Made in the USA
Columbia, SC
11 August 2024

40354074R00113